Fall in Love Like a Romance Writer

AMELIA GREY

Health Communications, Inc.
Deerfield Beach, Florida

www.hcibooks.com

Library of Congress Cataloging-in-Publication Data

Grey, Amelia.
 Fall in love like a romance writer / Amelia Grey.
  p. cm.
 ISBN-13: 978-0-7573-1554-1
 ISBN-10: 0-7573-1554-2
 1. Man-woman relationships. 2. Marriage. I. Title.
 HQ801.G727 2011
 305.3—dc22

2010047690

©2010 Gloria Skinner

All rights reserved. Printed in the United States of America. No part of this publication may be reproduced, stored in a retrieval system, or transmitted in any form or by any means, electronic, mechanical, photocopying, recording, or otherwise, without the written permission of the publisher.

HCI, its logos, and marks are trademarks of Health Communications, Inc.

Publisher: Health Communications, Inc.
 3201 S.W. 15th Street
 Deerfield Beach, FL 33442–8190

Cover design by Larissa Hise Henoch
Interior design and formatting by Lawna Patterson Oldfield

This book is dedicated to
my husband, Floyd, with love,
for the past, the present,
and for the future.

Contents

Introduction 1

Secret Key #1: *Humor*

Robyn Carr The Secret to a Long and Silly Marriage 6
Mariah Stewart My Hero 9
Annette Blair Reader, I Married Him 13
Wendy Corsi Staub How an Office Party
  "Don't" Led to "I Do" 18
Victoria Alexander How I Got to Happily Ever After
  and Stayed There 22
Stef Ann Holm A Very Special Feeling 26
Susan Andersen How to Beat the Odds 29
Amanda McCabe Never Marry a Man Who Can't
  Make You Laugh 32
Teresa Medeiros The Girl of His Choice 35

Secret Key #2: *Moonstruck*

Julianne MacLean Swept Away 40
Elizabeth Grayson Once Upon a Red Light 45
Judi Fennell Love at First Sight 49
Bertrice Small He's the One 54
Amanda Scott Then, Now, and Always 58
Jennifer Blake A Romantic Dreamer 62

Jo Ann Ferguson Some (Less Than) Enchanted Evening 64
Michele Ann Young A Knight on a White Steed 68
Nicola Cornick Best Mistake I Ever Made 71
Kasey Michaels I Want Him 74
Eloisa James How I Found True Love 78

Secret Key #3: *Inspiration*

Pamela Morsi Lightning Strikes Twice 82
Kate Austin Smacked by Fate 87
Deb Stover Our Hero 91
Sabrina Jeffries The Love of My Life 95
Gayle Callen Finding Love in the Most Unlikely Place 98
Mary Jo Putney Love: In Sickness and in Health 101
Cathy Maxwell The Most Dangerous Thing 104

Secret Key #4: *Opposites Attract*

Jean Brashear Celebrate Your Differences 110
Meryl Sawyer It's Not What You Say but How You Say It 114
Shirl Henke First Dates Can Last a Lifetime 118
Lorraine Heath The Realist and the Dreamer 122
Heather Graham Falling in Love Is Easy;
    Staying in Love Is Hard Work 127
Shana Galen Sports Are Stranger Than Fiction 132
Stella Cameron Loving Is the Answer 136
Linda Wisdom Falling in Love 140
Jill Marie Landis Exceptional Moments of Love 143
Elizabeth Boyle When Opposites Attract 147

Geri Buckley Borcz What About Opposites?..................151
Mary Balogh In the Nick of Time.................................154
Kat Martin For Better or Worse 158
Jasmine Cresswell A Romantic Moment........................161

Secret Key #5: *Second Chances*

Barbara Samuel A View from the Top of the World..................166
Nicole Byrd Happy Endings...171
Elizabeth Hoyt The Opposite of Love at First Sight...................175
Ciji Ware A Marriage of Long Duration...........................177

Secret Key #6: *Trust and Respect*

Rachel Gibson Friends and Lovers.................................182
Gaelen Foley Show, Don't Tell.....................................185
Linda Lael Miller A Hero You Can Trust.........................188
Jannine Corti Petska Romance Is Calling: Don't Hang Up.......190
Joan Johnston Thoughtfulness Is the Key 195
Stephanie Bond How Do You Spell R-O-M-A-N-C-E?..........197
Cheryl Brooks He's Still the One..................................199
Patricia Potter Respect Keeps Romance Alive..................202
Sharon Lathan My Own Mr. Darcy..............................204
Judith Arnold Three Thousand Miles 207
Karen Robards For the Long Haul................................210
Suzanne Forster Who's the Boss? 212
Karen White A Match Made at Wimbledon....................218

Secret Key #7: *Hope*

Jane Porter Forty and Fabulous 224

Dee Davis True Love 227

Robin Lee Hatcher A More Excellent Way 232

Jade Lee The Walk to the Roof 235

Haywood Smith The Greatest Love 239

Terry Spear The Elements of Love 242

Leigh Greenwood Worth the Effort 244

Christie Ridgway Picture This 247

Laura Lee Guhrke In Praise of Younger Men 250

Afterword: Faith, Hope, and Love 253

Acknowledgments 256

Introduction

Isn't it wonderful when a tremendously brilliant idea flashes through our brains? That's how the concept for this book came to me—in a dazzling moment of "Wouldn't it be wonderful if the women who write about fictional love every day told their readers their very own love story?"

What could be more fascinating, and more inspiring than to read about the true romances of some of America's most beloved romance authors?

But could I do it? Where and how would I start?

I have been a romance author for twenty years and during that time I've made a lot of friends, but did I dare ask these beautiful and dedicated women who write fictional happily-ever-after stories to write something for me about their personal and private lives? And, if I could by some chance entice the authors I knew to help me with this intriguing idea, would I then be able to persuade some authors I didn't know?

While the idea of such a book appealed to me, the task itself seemed daunting, impossible.

Time passed but my desire to work on this book didn't. If anything, the longer I put it off, the more I wanted to do it.

But before I could ask my friends to help me with this project, I had to write my own story. So I began:

The first time I saw him, he was leaning against the fender of a sporty, 1965 canary yellow Comet Cyclone holding a thin cigar. Surprising I know, considering he was a senior in high school and not a well-seasoned man about town, but true. Thankfully smoking didn't become a habit for him, but looking at him that late Sunday afternoon with smoke curling up from his fingers made my seventeen-year-old heart thump loud enough to cause a roar in my temples. One thing was for sure. He wasn't from around our small town. That golden-eyed, brown-haired hunk dressed in tight jeans and a light-blue button-down collared shirt had the appeal of the all-American bad boy, and I couldn't believe my good fortune when he threw down the cigar, walked over to my car, and said hello.

    Writing those few words describing how I met my husband made me feel the power of that moment all over again, and gave me the confidence I needed to press forward with the dream that was never far from my thoughts. It also made me realize that I not only wrote about the fictional happily-ever-after life, I was living the true happily-ever-after life. And so were many of my author friends. So, denying my fear of mass rejections, I sent out e-mails asking if they would be willing to write a few words about how they met the love of their lives, or how they made their love last through the years. For my friends who didn't have a current love in their lives, I asked what they believed made love and romance timeless. To my surprise, I received a resounding yes from almost every author I contacted.

    My journey then began in earnest to add other authors to the list and find the hidden secrets that led to lasting love and commitment.

In this book, one author says the greatest gift her husband ever gave her was a baseball glove. Another explains how a sudden, life-threatening illness brought her and her husband closer together. One author vowed she'd never marry a man like her father, and then fell head over heels in love with a man just like her father. And yet another author tells why she embroidered her husband's name in the band of all his underwear. Some of the stories are heartwarming, some are inspiring, and others are filled with humor, but they are all sprinkled with the magical feeling of love.

This collection of over sixty love stories is filled with icons such as Bertrice Small and Jennifer Blake, who helped define romance books as we know them today, and many of romance's newest stars. All of the stories are different, but while reading them, I realized that some of the same themes kept appearing: opposites attracting, being moonstruck, the offering of hope, finding inspiration, keeping humor, and the embodiment of trust. If these words kept appearing it must mean that they were important to an enduring and successful relationship. I started thinking of them as The Secret Keys to a Fulfilling and Lasting Love. So sit back, relax, and enjoy these incredible and intimate secrets about love from your favorite romance writers.

Oh, and, as for that good-looking bad boy from just across the state line? We married shortly after graduating from high school. He was nineteen and I was a mere eighteen years old. Right from the start, our youth put three strikes against us when it came to staying together for any length of time, but you'll read more about our story at the end. It's time to get on to the celebrities and let them share their stories of love with you.

Secret Key #1

Humor

LUCK PLAYS A PART IN ANY MARRIAGE BUT I THINK A SENSE OF HUMOR AND A WILLINGNESS TO COMMUNICATE ASSUME MORE IMPORTANT ROLES. IF YOU RECOGNIZE THE ABSURDITY OF A SITUATION AND REFUSE TO TAKE YOURSELF TOO SERIOUSLY OR TO THINK THAT YOURS IS THE ONLY OPINION THAT COUNTS, CHANCES ARE THAT MORE DISAGREEMENTS THAN NOT WILL STAY OUT OF THAT NO-WIN TERRITORY WHERE YOU FIND YOURSELF DEFENDING POSITIONS NOT PARTICULARLY WORTHY OF A DEFENSE.

—*Susan Andersen*

Robyn Carr
The Secret to a Long and Silly Marriage

This is an absolutely true story—not a single embellishment, I swear. A friend of mine, also a writer, was conducting a survey. She was asking people who had been married at least a couple of decades what one word they would use to describe the secret of a successful marriage. A big romance writers' conference was a perfect lab for her experiment—she asked the question over and over. When she asked me, "Humor," popped out of my mouth before I could stop it. A stunned look came over her and she said she'd never heard that one before. The obvious words had come up again and again—commitment, compromise, loyalty, patience, forgiveness, sacrifice, unselfishness, friendship. Never humor.

I can't disagree with any of those other things; all are obviously necessary. I felt a little embarrassed. Maybe silly and shallow. Did this mean I couldn't make all those other things work unless I was having fun?

"Will you do me a favor?" she asked me. "When you get home, will you ask your husband for his one word and e-mail it to me?"

I had no problem with that, certain he'd have more sense than me. When I did finally remember to ask him, his word was,

"Humor!" My turn for my mouth to fall open in surprise. In my shock that this could actually happen, that both of us could come up with the same word, I decided that we'd lasted because we think alike. Or maybe we're both just a couple of goofs who find things like rotten teenagers, overdue mortgages, broken down cars, unemployment, and pesky, interfering in-laws funny!

I do remember starting one Christmas letter with, "The children are trying to kill us. . . ." And there was this time a neighbor gave me a jar of chlorine "shock" for the pool and I lifted the lid and gave it a sniff—after which I keeled over and my husband had to call Poison Control to find out if I was going to expire. He kneeled over me and said that my nose and throat would be very sore for a few hours, but I wasn't in danger of dying. And he added, "But, you did kill a lot of perfectly good brain cells and will be dumb as a stump for a couple of weeks." Only a total goof makes fun of a dying woman.

Looking back over decades, while we've clung fearfully and a little helplessly to all those other things—the commitment and compromise, et cetera, at the end of the day, someone almost always cracks wise. It may not come in the middle of a crisis or even immediately following, it may not come during a big disagreement, but one of us always slings a funny. And it lightens the load.

Because there's always a load. Life is hard; relationships are complex. Love is a mystery. Family life can be a minefield.

And maybe laughter is the best medicine after all. Didn't Norman Cousins cure himself of a terminal disease by watching Laurel and Hardy and Three Stooges films?

The funniest Christmas letter we ever received was from a dear friend who described scattering his father's ashes on the lake, having them blow back in their faces and into the boat, vacuuming up most of dear old Dad and ending with, "Dad would've loved it!" I think I had more admiration for my friend and his family from that letter than any other long, serious tribute I have ever known.

We have to work at a lot of things to have a successful marriage. But in the end if we can say we had a good time, I guess there's not a thing wrong with that. And who knows, it might be the secret pill!

Robyn Carr is the RITA Award winning, *New York Times* bestselling author of forty novels, including the critically acclaimed Virgin River series. She lives with her husband in Las Vegas, Nevada. You can visit Robyn at www.robyncarr.com.

Mariah Stewart

My Hero

It was 1976 and I was living alone for the first time in my life. My apartment was in a three-story Victorian house in a small town outside of Philadelphia. The downstairs apartment was inhabited by a lovely, slightly older woman and the third floor by the most laid-back, casual guy I'd ever met. The three of us became good friends. I'd been handling all my own little day-to-day things quite well, I thought, and had come to believe I could handle anything on my own.

Well, anything that doesn't involve rodents or crawly things.

I'd come home from work one stormy evening to find a small black and white kitten huddled on the front porch. She was cute and wet and followed me into the foyer the second I pushed the door open. Well, what could I do? I invited her in. She kept in step with me all the way up the stairs to my second-floor apartment. She wore no collar, had no tags, and made herself at home in my apartment.

I let her out with me the next morning, thinking she'd find her way home, but when I returned that night she was there, waiting. I named her Tinker and bought her dry food and a litter box and other cat paraphernalia, and she moved in for good. Then one night while I was watching TV, I heard a crash from the kitchen. I ran in to investigate and found Tinker hunched over in the corner. I picked her up, wondering if she'd hurt herself somehow, but she kept her head averted, as if hiding something. I turned that cat this way and that, but she wouldn't let me see her face. Finally, as if to say, "Well, okay, but just remember, you asked for it!" she swung her head around so I could see . . . the head of a MOUSE hanging out one side of her mouth, and the tail dangling from the other!

Well, of course, I screamed and tossed the cat into the living room, ran down the hall, out the door, and up the steps. Wayne, I thought, would know what to do. Wayne would help me to get the cat out of the apartment.

I raced to his door and banged, yelling his name, two obvious signs, I thought, of distress.

"You have to help me!" I grabbed onto the front of his shirt. "Tinker caught a mouse, and I . . ."

"Who's Tinker?" he asked as if I were not all but foaming at the mouth.

"My cat, and she's . . ."

"When did you get a cat?"

"What difference does it make? She's in my apartment with a mouse!"

Right about this point, a guy stepped into the hallway. He was tall and had a fringe of brown hair that fell over his forehead, very blue eyes, and a very nice build. I'd seen him once or twice in passing, and though we hadn't met, I knew he was a friend of Wayne's from high school.

"Where's the cat now?" Handsome Stranger asked.

"She was in the living room," I told him.

"Is your apartment door open?"

"It's unlocked." Still hyperventilating, I followed him down the steps cautiously. "But I closed it so she wouldn't follow me."

He went into my apartment while I waited outside, hanging over the railing and ready to run if need be. But he emerged a minute later with Tinker—mouse still dangling—and very calmly took both outside.

I don't know what happened to the mouse, and sometime later circumstances forced me to part with Tinker (who ended up living on a farm outside of Cranbury, New Jersey, with author Rita Mae Brown), but my hero and I married two years later. Our daughters have carried on the family tradition of calling on him whenever danger threatens.

"Daddy! There's a spider in my room!"

"Dad! There's a bat in the hallway!"

"Dad, there's a snake out by the pool!"

Last week, it was me: "Bill! There are a whole bunch of yellow jackets in my office!"

Bill showed up with the vacuum cleaner and sucked 'em all up.

And just yesterday, there I was, yelling from the back door: "Bill! One of the dogs caught something in the backyard and it's furry and I don't really want to know what it is!"

And so, thirty-one years later—he's still my hero.

Mariah Stewart is the award-winning, *New York Times* bestselling author of twenty-eight novels of contemporary romance and romantic suspense. A native of Hightstown, New Jersey, she lives amid the rolling hills and Amish farms of southern Chester County, Pennsylvania, with her husband and their dogs, where she gardens, reads, and dreams up her next novels. She is currently working on the next book in her bestselling Chesapeake Diaries series. Please visit her website at www.mariahstewart.com.

Annette Blair
Reader, I Married Him

It is a fact universally acknowledged that any boy who sits beside you in junior high must be a royal pain in the neck. For me, one was worse than the rest.

Robert Blair came to our school in sixth grade and sat in the next row, one desk behind me. He always made jokes to entertain the class and annoy the teacher. I was aware of him from day one, in that "He'll never make me turn to look at him" way. That didn't change in three years, but he did. Six feet tall by seventh grade, they had to put his desk in the back row, and they couldn't screw it to the floor or he wouldn't fit. Mostly, it sat on his knees.

He was late for school regularly, often without his uniform tie. The ongoing battle of wills between him and our teacher about that became class entertainment. If that nun went charging down the aisle first thing, we knew why. On the rare days he wore his tie, he wore it loose just to annoy her. On one occasion, she shoved that knot so fast, and so far up his neck, he turned beet red from lack of oxygen.

In eighth grade, I sat beside Mr. Blair for geography. He would ask me questions but I refused to talk in class. The way he tells it, I was an A student and he was *NOT*. I could add that I was a goody two shoes and he was not, but he surely had more fun that I did. During geography, he would stand his oversize book fanned open on his desk so he could nap behind it.

More than once, our teacher would say, "Ms. Lague, is Mr. Blair asleep again?" Mortified, I would look in his direction. "Yes, Sister," I'd say with a sigh. I can tell you right now that it's a blessing we don't know our futures in advance.

We went to different schools after that. Once during that time, a car stopped to let me cross the street. *That's Robert Blair from the eighth grade*, I remember thinking of the driver, but I didn't think he'd remember me, so I didn't wave.

A few years later, I planned to become a nun, but because I had an ulcer I had to wait a year to enter the convent. During that time, a friend set me up on a blind date. Sure, his name gave me a jolt, but the description didn't fit. An hour before my date arrived, I told my mother to tell him I was sick and couldn't go out.

My mother, bless her, said, "If you don't want to go, you tell him." Face-to-face in my parents' parlor I realized I was going out with the pain. He had matured incredibly well—read: thoughtful, a gentleman, drop-dead gorgeous. We went to a movie: *The Sound of Music*. Later at dinner, he admitted that he was always as aware of me as I had been of him, but he admitted it first. He worked out of state at the time and only came home on weekends, so we left it that he'd call me the following Friday night. I dressed for a date.

He didn't call. Ah, well, not meant to be. I put on my homemade nightgown, constructed from a grain-bag from my grandparents' farm, curled my hair in pink rollers, and added a layer of Desitin to my face. Can you say, "scary ghost"?

I was watching TV when someone knocked at the door. My mother let him in too fast for me to escape. He had to work late, so he came to apologize for not calling. I'm looking like zombie woman in headlights, and he asks if I want to go out the next night. I mumbled a *yes*, ate up his smile, and he left. I was still in shock, standing in the middle of the room, through which, I later learned, the shadow from the TV gave away my silhouette. "Ah," I eventually asked him, "so you weren't looking at my face that night." "Well," he said. "That was beautiful, too." He was so not looking at my face.

On the first anniversary of our first date, we saw *The Sound of Music* again. We had been married for two weeks by then. We've now been married four decades and have two children and several grands to enhance our love. On a recent Sunday, Mr. Blair woke me up. He said, "No writing today. I packed us a picnic, and the Blairmobile is leaving in an hour." We went to Cape Cod, enjoyed antiquarian bookstores and antique shops, and at sunset, we snuggled on West Dennis Beach and ate our picnic supper while the sky did a lightshow you can't imagine. Is it any wonder that I write romance?

Of course we're normal and we don't always agree, but fights usually end in laughter because we know each other so well. Those things about your new husband that annoy you so much? If you make it as far as we did, you'll smile and think, *how cute*.

The awareness I once felt for the new kid in sixth grade has deepened profoundly. Eternal love, it's called. He's the center of my world, my heart's beat. He supports me in my writing and has never let me clean the snow off my own car. He's Poppy to a little one who accepts his hand as the ultimate protection. Smart girl. He's my life, my lover, my best friend, the person I laugh with in every aspect of our life together, the one whose hand feels like silk in mine, and whose arms open before I realize I need them.

It's not always easy to recognize your soul mate, but if it's meant to be, fate will find a way. I'm grateful for that. *The Sound of Music* never comes on that we don't snuggle, hold hands, and relive that first magical date.

As an aside, our daughter attended the college owned by the nuns we had in grammar school, the order I nearly entered. She had some of the same teachers, and you know, they remembered the royal pain better than the goody two-shoes. Even nuns love a bad boy.

Photo by Edward Tenczar

Annette Blair—National bestselling, award-winning author Annette Blair owes her paranormal roots to Salem, Massachusetts, where she stumbled into the serendipitous role of Accidental Witch Writer. Magic or destiny, her bewitching romantic comedies became national bestsellers. Contracted to Book 31, Annette is now writing both her Works like Magick novels and Vintage Magic mysteries. Please visit her website at www.annetteblair.com.

Wendy Corsi Staub

How an Office Party "Don't" Led to "I Do"

New York City, December 12, 1988: I'd just celebrated my twenty-fourth birthday and had been working since August at Backer Spielvogel Bates, one of Manhattan's biggest advertising agencies. This was the tail end of the industry's boom era: bottomless expense accounts, martini lunches, lavish parties, perks galore.

The agency went all out for the annual holiday party that year, renting an entire nightclub, Dezerland, for an evening of open bar and dancing.

My best work-friend Jennie and I had recently read a magazine article about being a "Do" and a "Don't" at the office Christmas party, and that night, we fell squarely into the "Don't" category. We arrived early, stayed late, drank cocktails, danced, gossiped, and dressed provocatively (my attire: big earrings, big hair, dramatic makeup, heels, a black spandex miniskirt, and some kind of off-the-shoulder red top–it was the '80s, remember? I was channeling my inner "Simply Irresistible"-Robert Palmer–video girl).

Had I been an office party "Do," I'm sure I never would have met my future husband. Mark, like most single guys his age, thought a "Don't" was a lot more fun.

He worked in the media department, and I was in account management. The company was huge, having recently gone through a merger and a move to new offices straddling the Chrysler Building and the adjacent Kent Building, which explains why we had never set eyes on each other until that night. We hadn't even worked under the same roof.

I had, however, unwittingly set eyes on his wardrobe. At least, part of it. Whenever my boss wore a great tie, I'd compliment it and think that he was full of surprises—he wasn't particularly a fun-tie kind of guy. Little did I know that he had a roommate who was.

Said roommate arrived late at the party, being an integral (MVP) member of the company's volleyball team, which had just played a match. He then found himself being lectured by his female boss (and good pal) about the fact that he was only interested in dating around, and never had long-term relationships (not, mind you, that he thought *that* was a problem). "You always go after the wrong kind of woman," she said. "Women like . . ." (looking around the room, she zeroed in on slutty-looking *moi*, and pointed) ". . . her."

He took one glance and made a beeline over, assuming a nice, shallow fling would ensue. When he introduced himself to me with a "Hi, I'm Mark," I was in the midst of posing for Jennie's camera with my fellow "Don't" friends. I said (or perhaps shrieked), "You have to get into the piiiictuuuure!" Thus, we posed together for a snapshot, capturing our seconds-old relationship forever on film.

Then Mark took the camera and turned it toward us both for one of his famous "chin shots" (of which there would be many more to come over the next two decades).

Later that night, I learned that he was my boss's roommate—the source of all those great ties—and he learned I wasn't actually a slut as implied by my "Don't" outfit. He stuck around anyway.

As the party heated up, we danced to "I've Had the Time of My Life," never imagining that a literal interpretation was in our future. Still later, while having a nightcap at the Flatiron district bar Live Bait, I accidentally knocked an entire beer into his lap, soaking his suit. He actually laughed it off. We went our separate ways in cabs, but he had my phone number in his pocket. He called the next morning.

In the bright, sober light of day, I decided it might not be a great idea to date my boss's roommate—much less, to have hung all over him at the company party the night before. At lunchtime, I put on big dark sunglasses and slunk out of the Chrysler Building and down 42nd Street to seek counsel from my wise friend Lucia, an editor at Harlequin-Silhouette (yes, romance novels).

"Look at it this way," she said, "if you marry the guy in a few years, everyone will think the way you met was really romantic, and if you don't, by then they'll have forgotten all about it anyway."

She was right.

P.S. I married the guy twenty years ago.

P.P.S. In 2004, Harlequin-Silhouette published *Slightly Settled*, the chick-lit novel I wrote under the pseudonym Wendy

Markham, about a twenty-something Office Christmas Party Don't who meets Mr. Right.

Wendy Corsi Staub has published more than seventy novels, including a number of *New York Times* best sellers. Her latest, *Live to Tell*, launches a trilogy and received a starred *Publishers Weekly* review. Her YA paranormal series Lily Dale is optioned by Freemantle Productions. Alter-ego Wendy Markham writes bestselling chick lit. Please visit her website at www.wendycorsistaub.com.

Victoria Alexander

How I Got to Happily Ever After and Stayed There

I asked him out.

Yep, that's how it started more than—as much as I hate to admit it—thirty years ago. I guess time really does fly when you're having fun. But that's the end of the story.

As for the beginning . . .

My husband Chuck and I worked at the same television station. He was in production and I was in news. We had done really well in the ratings so the news staff was being treated to a night out at a very nice restaurant. The guy I was currently dating was out of town. Chuck was a production assistant so I asked him if he wanted to come with me. I didn't say *as friends* but that's what I meant. Well, all week everyone teased him about our "date." I kept telling him I would expect flowers at the very least. So when he came to pick me up, he had a tiny basket filled with miniature pink roses. Needless to say, I was hooked. I still have the basket.

I knew in less than two weeks that this was the guy I'd spend the rest of my life with. How did I know? I have no idea but I knew. Two years later we were married.

Because I write romance, I'm often asked for my advice about love and marriage. As a writer, I'm not sure my advice is valid. After all, I write fiction. I make it all up.

But ask for advice based on my real-life relationship of more than thirty years and I can go on for hours.

In fiction, I think a perfect hero needs a certain amount of arrogance, a sense of humor, and a really nice butt. In real life, I think a man you're going to spend the rest of your life with needs to have the qualities of a hero. My husband does.

In terms of arrogance, he thinks he's always right. But then so do I, and I am stubborn enough not to admit when I'm wrong. I need my mistakes pointed out to me. He's willing to do that. It drives me crazy. But then my obstinate nature drives him crazy. It's a balancing act.

As for a sense of humor, well, you have to have one to live with me. But then I need one to live with him, too. He's never read one of my books. He's a nonfiction rather than a fiction reader. But since he doesn't read my books, I started naming dead husbands after him in about my third book. It's become a tradition. When I have a dead husband in a book, and he wasn't evil or a bad guy, I name him Charles. I have dead Charleses now in most of my books. At first, when he realized I named heroes after old boyfriends and dead husbands after him, he was a little annoyed. Now, he's annoyed if I don't name dead husbands after him.

I think it keeps our marriage fresh. He thinks it keeps him safe. He's mentioned more than once that if anything happened to him I'd be the first suspect. He takes a great deal of comfort from that. And I like keeping him on his toes.

I won't talk about the nice butt part. You'll have to trust me on that.

Probably my best advice about marriage is to give each other space. You don't have to do everything together. There are a lot of things he likes doing that I don't and vice versa, so we do them separately. (Oh sure, he did once take disco lessons for me and I did play soccer for him, but we've grown since then.) He gets together with his friends, I go to conferences with mine. But at the end of the day, or the end of the road, we always have the other to come back to.

And you know, after all these years, we can still make each other laugh. That's important, too.

Your best friend doesn't need to be your true love but your true love should also be your best friend. My husband is my best friend. And my hero. When I am in the midst of crisis, he's there. Always.

And yeah, I think he's my soul mate.

So, just like the characters in my books, I'm living happily ever after.

I am lucky and I know it. Don't tell him though. That, too, keeps him on his toes.

Photo by Dawn Biggs

Victoria Alexander is the #1 *New York Times* bestselling author of more than thirty published works. A former broadcast journalist, she lives in Omaha, Nebraska, with two bearded collies and her long-suffering husband. They laugh a great deal. They have to. Please visit her website at www.victoriaalexanderbooks.com.

Stef Ann Holm
A Very Special Feeling

My husband and I have only been married a few years, and we're still enjoying the honeymoon phase of our new life. This is a second marriage for both of us after long-term first marriages. Since we were older when we met, our habits and routines had settled into place, and the easy-going days of our early twenties were a distant memory.

As we got to know each other, dating became a new journey, and we soon realized that it was fun to be spontaneous. On warm summer evenings we'd jump on his motorcycle and ride around town with no destination in mind. Winter nights, we'd go to a movie that started at midnight and not care how late it would get out. We just wanted to spend time together. We still do, and it's so nice to help him with projects or surprise him with random acts of kindness. He really appreciates it.

My husband is a very romantic man. I've found love notes from him in the most unlikely places—under the lid of my coffee creamer or laying inside the washing machine to thank me for doing his laundry. Once, he used pink nail polish to write "I love you" on my bathroom mirror. And I didn't just fall in love with his romantic ways; he's also kind, generous, and patient, and has a sense of humor that keeps me laughing.

Everyone who knows him knows that deep and hearty laugh of his!

I enjoy dropping a little sense of humor in my husband's life, and when I do, I try my best to make *him* laugh.

As part of his giving nature, he came home one day with a new professional sewing machine for me. He proudly presented it and declared my old 1976 Kenmore should be retired. The new machine runs by a computer . . . it'll be a while before I figure it all out. But in the interim, I decided to test the embroidery feature and embroidered my husband's first name on all the elastic bands of his underwear. The following day, he discovered my handiwork, briefs folded neatly in his drawer with the name facing out, and hasn't stopped laughing since. I don't think it's *that* funny, but he's gotten a lot of mileage out of it, telling everyone what I did. (And I mean everyone!)

So for us, loving each other has a lot of humor in it, but also thoughtfulness as well. When he goes on a business trip, I always try to slip a greeting card in his overnight bag so he can open it. Once after he'd had a long day working in the yard, I had a cold beer on the shower shelf waiting for him. He loved that.

I truly think a lasting romance starts with a man and a woman willing to put their loved one before themselves. While our lives get busy and it sometimes seems a chore to go out of your way, just do it and make your man feel special. It will go a long way.

I'm so happy I have that special feeling each day when I wake up and the coffee is made for me and my creamer is sitting out next to the heart-coffee cup my sweetie bought for me. To me, that's a great way to start my morning—and better yet, to live my life!

Photo by Nick Miller

USA Today bestselling author **Stef Ann Holm** lives in Boise, Idaho, with her husband and family. She has two beautiful daughters, and a Yorkie who stalks squirrels. She loves hot summers, sunshine, sitting poolside in her backyard, and traveling. Her latest passion is BSU Football—Go Broncos! Visit her website at www.stefannholm.com.

Susan Andersen

How to Beat the Odds

I've been married nearly forty-two years. The soul mate and I met when we were just sixteen and seventeen. We attended different high schools, so might have never crossed paths, except in my sophomore year a boy who was dating a friend of mine got it into his head that he couldn't rest until he hooked me up with one of his buds.

The first guy he introduced me to was twenty-five years old. Hello! Did you get the part where I was sixteen? If I'd been twenty-six and Mr. Hook-up thirty-five, the age differences might not have seemed so huge. As it was, I told him my mother was calling (I lived across the street) and ran, did not walk, right out the door.

I struck gold with the second guy he brought to meet me. That would be my honey, of course. Now *he* had it going on all levels.

We married way too young (nineteen and twenty), yet somehow managed to beat the odds stacked against teen marriages. Over the years, we've loved each other, raised each other, and when all is said and done (which, okay, thankfully it's not yet) have laughed together far more often than we've fought.

Luck plays a part in any marriage, but I think a sense of humor and a willingness to communicate assume more important roles.

It's important to recognize the absurdity of a situation and refuse to take yourself too seriously or to think that yours is the only opinion that counts. Chances are, more disagreements than not will stay out of that no-win territory where you find yourself defending positions not particularly worthy of a defense. My husband is a quiet man and can be reserved at times. But he has a sense of humor that just tickles me pink and makes me laugh every day we're together. Not only is that a huge aphrodisiac, it motivates me in putting my own continued effort into our relationship.

I swear, though, it's the little things that can rub a marriage raw. The two of us have always powered through the bigger problems. But those minor irritations that can sometimes pile up, one on top of the other, are what make the separations that are the norm in our life not necessarily a bad thing. In fact, they can be downright handy.

The soul mate's an engineer who spends a great deal of time in the field doing start-ups around the globe. All that travel can be a pain at times. But it can also be a blessing. For just when the little every day, familiarity-breeds-contempt annoyances begin to wear our nerves thin, he has to leave for another job. Some trips are as short as a couple of days, while others take him away for as long as three months. Regardless, the end result is the same. By the time he gets home again, the aggravations that had assumed way more importance than they warranted no longer matter. Instead, we have a shiny new appreciation for each other.

It's a lifestyle that might not appeal to everyone, but it works for us. And that's probably the secret to most workable marriages: they don't have to be what anyone else considers viable.

They only have to do the trick for you.

Photo by Studio B Portraits

Susan Andersen writes contemporary romance with an edge of suspense and humor to keep things interesting. Her books have spent many weeks on the *New York Times, USA Today,* and *Publishers Weekly* bestseller lists, and since 2001 have been an annual inclusion in the Amazon Editors' Top Ten Best Of list. The proud mama of a grown son who will forever remain her Sweet Baby Boy, Sue is a native of the Pacific Northwest, where she lives with her husband and two cats. Please visit her website at www.susanandersen.com.

Amanda McCabe

Never Marry a Man Who Can't Make You Laugh

I write about love and romance every day, creating characters who meet, fall in love, build a relationship, and end by promising to commit to each other and be together forever, no matter what may come. (Though getting to this point never runs smoothly, of course!) I love creating heroes and heroines who are perfect for each other and then seeing how they work things out together. But when people ask me how to keep romance alive in *real* life—that's not quite as clear and easy! I guess if I knew that answer, I could write self-help books as well as novels. . . .

Myself, I like the usual things—flowers, Godiva chocolates, trips to Paris (what could be more romantic than a picnic by the Eiffel Tower?), "date nights" to make time just for each other. Being engaged in each other's lives and remembering to be kind and supportive, even when it's not an easy thing. Laughing together. Building memories.

I think I learned all this from my grandparents. They were married for almost sixty years, having met when they were teenagers. After decades together, five children, countless moves and crises moments and everyday living, they still kissed in the kitchen. They held hands watching TV, laughed at silly old "in" jokes, and enjoyed every minute with the family they built together. Sometimes they would quarrel (especially when driving—my grandfather always got lost and always refused to ask for directions), but it would always end with laughter and another kiss. My grandmother always told me to never marry a man who doesn't make you laugh!

They are both gone now, but remembering their love and commitment, and how much they appreciated every day together, still makes me smile. I also see their inspiration in my parents, who are soon to have their fortieth anniversary!

I haven't yet found my perfect match as they did, but I'm doing as my grandmother advised—I'm waiting for a man who makes me laugh. And a trip to Paris to kiss by the Seine wouldn't be so bad, either. . . .

Photo by Cara Koenig

Amanda McCabe, aka Laurel McKee, writes historical romance for Harlequin Historicals and Grand Central Publishing. She lives in Oklahoma, surrounded by books, antiques, and a menagerie of dogs and cats. You can visit her at www.ammandamccabe.com and www.laurelmckee.net.

Teresa Medeiros
The Girl of His Choice

My husband and I met in a mental institution. Wait! Perhaps I should clarify that. My husband asked me out for the first time in a mental institution. But neither of us were patients. We were both nursing students doing our psychiatric clinical rotations. I was standing in front of the vending machines in the canteen when he came up and asked, "Would you like to go see the Hall & Oates concert? I'll pay for the gas if you'll buy the tickets." Needless to say, after such a romantic declaration, I could only think, "This . . . *this* is the man I want to spend the rest of my life with!"

But alas, it was not to be because I already had a boyfriend! I'd been dating the proverbial "bad boy" for three years, since the tender age of seventeen. During that time I'd turned down lots of nice offers from lots of nice boys. So after an evening of thoughtful consideration (during which my "bad boy" boyfriend stood me up for the last time), I decided that Michael Medeiros was one nice boy I just couldn't bear to turn down.

So I purchased the tickets to the Hall & Oates concert and handed them to Mike the very next day in an envelope marked "Take the girl of your choice." More than twenty years later, he still likes to tease me by asking what I would have done if he'd have taken some other girl to the concert. But I don't think he really wants to know!

Eight days after that first date (eight days, *not* eight dates), Mike said, "I love you" and I said "I love you back." I'd been a hopeless romantic who was perpetually in love since I was six years old, but even I knew this was something different. Something extraordinarily special. My heart lit up every time he walked into a room.

During our courtship phase, Mike inadvertently gave me one of the greatest gifts I would ever receive. When he told me he was bringing me a surprise, I had no idea what to expect. I was doubly surprised when he handed me a short story he had written in my honor. (Yes, I was the heroine and he was the hero.) Naturally, I did the only thing a woman could do under these touching circumstances—I took the story home and revised it. (What do you mean I was wearing a pink dress in that scene? I would never wear a pink dress! Why are you saving me from the villain here? I should be saving you!) The next day, I presented him with the neatly typed "revised" version of "his" story.

Prior to our meeting, I had pretty much lost my creative drive, but tinkering with his prose reminded me of just how much joy I derived from rearranging words on the page. Less than a year later, when I was twenty-one years old, I started working on what would become my first published novel *Lady of Conquest*.

Mike and I have been together for more than twenty-five years now and my heart still lights up every time he walks into the room. It's been a delight to share my life with a man who also shares my spiritual faith, my sense of humor, my appreciation for all things

Star Trek. We can laugh with each other and at each other. This is a man who swore he didn't like cats when we first got married . . . until he started bringing them home in his pockets. (We eventually ended up with five.) A man who has risked his life twice on medical and humanitarian trips to Haiti and Panama.

I'll never forget an Ann Landers letter I once read. A woman was writing to tell Ann her husband was never "overly affectionate." He didn't reach out for spontaneous hugs or hold her hand in public or say "I love you" with any regularity. But he made sure her car had regular tune-ups and every single week without fail, he brought her a bag of her favorite candy. It wasn't until his death, after thirty-five years of marriage, that she realized that every time he handed her that bag of candy, he was saying, "I love you." I thought of this at a convention we recently attended when I was sitting in a cold, drafty convention hall and my husband showed up with two things—my sweater and a bag of dark chocolate M&M's. I just smiled up at him and said, "I love you, too."

New York Times bestselling author **Teresa Medeiros** wrote her first novel at the age of twenty-one, introducing readers to one of the most beloved and versatile voices in romantic fiction. *Goodnight Tweetheart*, her novel about a man and woman who meet and fall in love on Twitter, was published in January 2011. You can visit her website at www.teresamedeiros.com.

Secret Key #2

Moonstruck

Do I believe in love at first sight? Maybe. I know I believe in instant attraction, I believe in your heart knowing something long before your mind and even your common sense begin to catch up. But what begins in giddiness and passion for each other can end just as swiftly if you don't work at keeping the love alive, and believe in sticking together when times get rough. You need to remember the love, always remember the love, even when Real Life gives it to you on the chin. It's still the love that comes first, the love that endures, the love that gets you through.

–Kasey Michaels

Julianne MacLean

Swept Away

I was eighteen years old when I first laid eyes on my husband, and in that moment, I was swept off my feet by a powerful ocean wave. Literally.

It was frosh week at university. I had chosen the same school as my high school boyfriend so that we could stay together. The day after we arrived, however, he took an interest in the first friend I made (oddly enough, he introduced us), and almost immediately they began a more intense "flirtation" that lasted the entire week and smashed my young hopeful heart into a thousand agonizing pieces.

By week's end I was an emotional wreck. I still cared for him, and it was excruciating to watch him waltz intimately with my new friend, right in front of me. On top of that, it was my first time living away from my family, so I felt completely lost and alone.

Thankfully, as the week unfolded, I met new friends—friends I could trust. They were supportive and sympathetic to my situation. (We remain close to this day, more than twenty-five years later.)

We all shared a blanket at the beach party, and while my boyfriend mingled elsewhere, I was soon targeted by a group of upperclassmen who were in charge of welcoming the first year students to the campus by throwing them into the frigid, foaming waters of the North Atlantic ocean.

It is an understatement to say I was not in the mood for such shenanigans. I had been fighting tears all day.

I fought hard when they scooped me off the blanket, but it was no use. It was frosh week after all. There were traditions to uphold.

Most of it was a blur after that. I remember flying through the air and splashing into the cold, crashing waves. Water flooded my ears and soaked through my clothes. I couldn't breathe. As I scrambled to my feet, coughing and sputtering, swaying against the pounding surf, I hyperventilated with shock and sobbing convulsions of heartache.

It was not a good day.

At least it didn't seem so at the time.

But now, looking back on it, I understand that it was the best day ever—because the first person I saw when I broke the surface and opened my eyes was my future husband.

He was the only one who stuck around long enough to make sure I hadn't drowned. The others had already taken off to snatch up the next unsuspecting freshman.

"Are you okay?" Stephen asked, looking concerned.

I'm not sure what I said. I suppose I nodded. I do remember that he walked me back to my blanket and chatted with my friends and me for a few more minutes before he returned to his duties.

From that moment on, I adored Stephen MacLean, the heroic

young gentleman who escorted me out of the water that day. He appears a number of times in the diaries I kept over the next three years while I completed my degree. (I once wrote: "Tonight I danced with Stephen MacLean! The song was 'Drive,' by The Cars.")

We were friends in university, but nothing more. It wasn't until five years after graduation that we bumped into each other in a video store on a Friday night. We were each alone, renting a movie. We stood in the action section and chatted for a long while. I recommended a film (it was *Jacob's Ladder*). He decided to rent it, but again, we went our separate ways.

Weeks later, we met at an informal college reunion in a local pub, and soon after, just like in any good romance novel, we fell in love. It was eight years after the first time I looked into his eyes, the day I was swept off my feet by that great ocean wave.

Today as I write this, we have been married for seventeen years. We are a perfect match. He is the great love of my life. We share the same family values and always treat each other with kindness and respect. We still watch movies on Friday nights, and he kisses me every day when he comes home from work. He also does dishes and laundry without my having to ask, and he supported me in my writing career, long before I was published.

He writes now, too. Not only does he help me brainstorm my own stories and proofread my work, in his spare time he works on screenplays. We have much in common, not to mention our beautiful daughter, who is the light of both our lives.

I firmly believe that happily ever after does exist in the real world, and real heroes walk among us.

My mother always told me to choose a husband with my head, not just my heart, and that is true as well. I knew intellectually that Stephen MacLean was a decent and kind man. I wouldn't have married him otherwise. That is why we have such a strong relationship. I respect him, I nurture our romance, and I never imagine that the grass is greener anywhere else.

I love the one I'm with, and that will never change.

Photo by Florian Kucheran

USA Today bestselling author **Julianne MacLean** has written numerous historical romances, including her popular American Heiress Series. She is a three time RITA Finalist with Romance Writers of America, and has won the Booksellers Best Award, the Colorado Romance Writer's prestigious Award of Excellence, a *Romantic Times* Reviewers' Choice Award, and grand prize winner for the More Than Magic Contest in 2004. She lives in Nova Scotia with her husband and daughter. Visit her website at www.juliannemaclean.com.

Elizabeth Grayson
Once Upon a Red Light

I could tell they were watching me.

I was stopped at a red light on a blustery Saturday night in downtown Rochester, New York. I was headed for an upscale bar called Shakespeare's to meet a guy I'd been dating for a couple of weeks. While I sat waiting for the light to change, two guys in a Mustang pulled up beside me.

Every woman with a pulse knows when a guy notices her. These two had and were obviously talking about me. Of course, I pretended to ignore them. When the light changed, I peeled out and left them eating my dust—the automotive equivalent of flipping my hair.

I didn't think much of it when I turned at the next corner and they followed me. I took some note when I turned two blocks later—and they followed me. My palms began to sweat when I turned into the underground garage where I had to park to catch the elevator to Shakespeare's—and they followed me.

With every warning my mom had ever given me about going out alone at night blaring in my head, I pulled the ticket and roared down into the garage. I sped down the ramps until I was able to park nose-to-doors with the elevator, and sat there shaking.

Was I taking a risk just getting out of the car? Should I drive home and call it a night? But then, George was waiting, and I refused to stand him up. So like a too-stupid-to-live heroine in a Gothic novel, I got out of the car and took the elevator.

George wasn't in Shakespeare's when I arrived, but the two guys from the red light were. Up close, they didn't look the least bit sinister.

The shorter one approached me. "Excuse me," he said, "I'm Michael. My friend and I thought we might have made you nervous by following you here, but we didn't know where we were going and it looked like you did. Can we buy you a drink to show our appreciation?"

Since there were at least a hundred other people in the room, I felt safe enough to agree. While we waited for our beverages, Michael introduced me to his friend Tom.

"I told Michael you were going to call the cops and have us arrested," Tom teased, giving me a dimpled smile.

"Well, I did consider making a citizen's arrest," I shot back.

I liked Tom right off. He was tall, broad-shouldered, with curly brown hair and blue eyes. When Michael wandered off, we found lots to talk about: we both worked in the arts and had friends in common. We read voraciously and liked the same books and movies. We both had dreams of world travel.

Midway through our conversation, George came in with a couple of the guys from work. Since I knew work was what they'd probably be talking about, I chatted with Tom a little longer. He was one of the nicest guys I'd ever met, smart, funny—and he made me a little breathless. So I couldn't help but be sorry when Michael came back and dragged him away.

George, when I went to join him, was furious that I had stayed and talked to Tom once he'd arrived.

"It was nothing," I assured him. "Just a conversation over a drink. He never even asked for my phone number."

I was more than a little disappointed about that. Tom was someone I wished I could have gotten to know better. Still, I'd been dating long enough to know that sometimes you got that special little tingle and the other person just didn't. Apparently Tom hadn't.

Or so I thought.

At the end of the evening when I went to my car, I found a note tucked under my windshield wiper. It read:

"Elizabeth—

I think you're fine.

Please call me at 555-6451.

Love—

Tom."

I called him, of course.

During the next year or so we dated. We fell in love. We got married.

I don't know if it was fate that brought us together at that red light, if it was the chance Tom took in leaving me that note that made everything else possible, or if I recognized something special in him the moment we met. What I do know is that I'm a lucky woman because we've been married for thirty-three years, and each has been better than the one before.

Elizabeth Grayson has published historical romances, series romance, and contemporary women's fiction. Her first historical romance won a coveted Waldenbook Award. She also received a Romantic Times Career Achievement Award for American Historical Fiction. She has twice made the honors list for the Willa Cather Literary Award and been a RITA finalist. What makes her happiest as a writer is leaving readers with a satisfied "Ah!" at the end of every story. Please visit her website at www.elizabethgrayson.com.

Judi Fennell

Love at First Sight

I grew up on fairy tales and every Disney movie there was, and started reading Romance in eighth grade. I wrote my first one in ninth. Not only did I want what those heroines had, but I believed in it, the whole thing: true love, love at first sight, lightning strikes, sweeping you off your feet, fireworks, happily ever after.

Why? Because I'm the third generation in my family to fall in love at first sight.

My grandparents met at a dance. My grandfather took one look at my grandmother and told her she was the prettiest girl he'd ever seen and he was going to marry her. Yep, first night.

But there was a problem: My grandmother had recently nursed her mother to the end of a terminal illness and her mother's greatest wish had been to see one of her daughters married. She never got that chance and my grandmother knew she couldn't handle wedding day emotions if she were a bride.

So, six weeks after the night they met, six weeks after my grandfather said he was going to marry her, my grandparents eloped. Their marriage lasted forty-nine years, until, as the vows say, "death do us part."

Twenty years later, my parents were set up by a mutual friend on a blind date. Dad had been engaged before, Mom had had several serious boyfriends; neither one was going into the date with blinders or rose-colored glasses on.

So you can imagine Mom's surprise, when, on date number three, Dad proposed. Four months later, they were married. (I, the oldest, was born two years after that, so we needn't go down that road.) Forty-seven years later, they're still together.

My own romance happened when I least expected it. You know how "they" say you get pregnant when you stop trying, or you find whatever it is you've lost when you stop looking, or the perfect man drops into your lap (nice!) when you finally stop searching? That's pretty much what happened to me.

My junior year in college was a big one. Since seventh grade, I'd planned and saved my money so I could participate in the Study Abroad program in Spain during spring semester. Now it was almost time, and it was all I focused on.

Okay, so maybe I wasn't focused on just the trip. I was, after all, in college, and parties were a nightly part of our lives. Several relationships had struck up and/or fizzled through the years from these parties.

But I'd decided that, as of November 1, I wasn't going to date anyone. I didn't want anything or anyone getting in the way of my spring semester and the planned three-month vacation afterward when my high school best friend and I would travel throughout Europe. This was my dream trip and I was going.

So guess what happened the night of November 1?

I'd been invited to a Halloween party and was dressed as a clown. And not just any clown, mind you, but a harlequin clown (talk about kismet)—you know, the type: white makeup with a tear on the cheek, white baggy shirt with black pom-poms, white pantaloons and cap? There was a popular series of posters of that clown in the '80s and I owned several.

So, there I was that evening in a hand-sewn costume made from my bed sheets and a skein of black yarn, chatting with a friend who was on her way out of the party. She didn't want to leave me standing there by myself, so she grabbed hold of some guy who was, literally, walking out of the party, and said, "Hey, dance with my friend."

"Some Guy" glanced at me and said, "Sure," waving goodbye to his buddies and trying to figure out if he had enough for cab fare home since buses didn't run to his apartment complex that late.

I've since asked this "Some Guy," now my husband, why he ever decided to ditch his ride for a chick in a clown costume. To this day, he still doesn't know. But he did and we spent hours dancing. He even swept me off my feet after I sprained my ankle.

Eleven days later, we had our first "official" date. Eight days after that, he told me he loved me, something he'd never said to anyone before me.

So here I was, less than two months from my trip of a lifetime and I was in love FOR REAL.

But I was going on that trip. I'd planned too long and sacrificed too much to earn the money for it. I was going.

Two AM on the day I was leaving, this "Some Guy" proposed to me over the phone. Eighteen hours before I was leaving for seven months.

Of course I said yes. Then I got on my plane and wondered if I'd done the right thing in going.

By the second week I was there, I knew I wouldn't make it the whole seven months. I didn't. I came home after classes were finished, leaving my best friend hanging. Am I proud of that? No. Would I do it differently if I could? Probably.

I knew he'd wait for me. He told me he would. He still says it, and I know it. But I was young and in love and you can't tell "those young kids" anything. So I came home and she went on the trip, plans slightly altered.

See, my friend had met an Egyptian guy in Paris on her Study Abroad program the year before, and decided to extend the week in Cairo we'd been planning on, to a month.

I'm sure you're thinking, "She came home engaged."

Actually, she didn't. She came home married. Twenty-four years later, they're still together.

But I'm thinking that a tour of the Europe I missed will make a nice anniversary trip some year—and number twenty-five is just around the corner.

Judi Fennell, winner of the PRISM Award, and author of a Mer series *(In Over Her Head, Wild Blue Under,* and *Catch of a Lifetime)*, and a Genie series (*I Dream of Genies, Genie Knows Best, Leave It to Genie*), enjoys hearing from her readers. Check out her website at www.JudiFennell.com.

Bertrice Small
He's the One

We all want love. Love as opposed to just sex. But how do we know when we've found love? Love, it seems, is a crapshoot at best. It usually happens when you least expect it. Here's how it happened to me.

For once I listened to my mother. And believe me that was a first. Like most respectable young women in the late '50s and early '60s I lived at home. Home was the upper East Side of Manhattan in NYC. I worked in broadcasting. As my twenty-fourth birthday approached I announced to my mother that I was giving myself a birthday party. In those days that meant a cocktail party. "Wonderful!" my mother said.

Then two girlfriends, and over a dozen young television and advertising guys showed up. My mother was not amused, especially when I told her I had deliberately invited only two girls, and lots of men. It was *my* birthday after all.

Shortly after that my mother began suggesting that I join the St. Bartholomew's Community Club. Actually she nagged a whole lot in tandem with her best friend, Jan Kirk. St. Bart's is the large and gorgeous Episcopal church built in the Byzantine style on Park Avenue in the '50s. Unlike most church groups for "young" people that seem to be filled with less than desirable types, and you all know what I mean, St. Bart's was overflowing with young professional men and women. They had lots of great activities, a fabulous theater group, a pool, and a cheap but good restaurant.

I complained to my old buddy, Ed Muller, about mom and Jan. Ed was the big brother I never had, and had known me since I was a kid. "Join," he said. "I'll sponsor you. I belong. This is a cool place, but you don't ever have to go if you don't want to go. Just join so Doris and Jan will shut up." So I did. Then promptly went off to Florida to visit cousins, and take my then ten-year-old goddaughter to Nassau in the Bahamas.

When I returned, Ed called and said the spring musical had been cast and they needed support staff. It would be a good way to meet a few people. So I stopped at the club after work on Wednesday, the ninth day of May 1962 where I was immediately snatched up by the props department to become the third assistant prop lady. And that same night Ed introduced me to his friend, George Small. The moment we met I knew this was the guy I had been waiting for my whole life.

I went home that same night and told my maternal grandmother, who lived with us, "Mary! I've just met the man I'm going to marry." "Good!" she said. "Bring him home to dinner, but let's wait till *they're* not here." "They," referring to my parents. Mary wanted the first look. She got it, and it was love at first sight. "He's the one," she agreed with me. There's a lesson here. Always trust your gut instinct where a man is concerned. And your favorite grandmother.

When my busy, professional parents finally met George

several months later they were concerned that he was fifteen years my senior. It was too late, however. We courted, and he proposed on Monday the twenty-sixth of August 1963. What did he say? From the moment he asked those words went out of my head, and I can't remember them to this day. I do remember asking him, "Are you kidding?" He laughed, and said no, he wasn't kidding.

He took me home then and spoke to my parents. My mother said to this forty-year-old man, "You do realize, George, that marriage is a very serious proposition?" George allowed that he did. My dad simply shook his hand, and welcomed him to the family. The next evening when he brought me home my mother had already gotten the envelopes for the invitations from Cartier and was addressing them. George teased her saying, "What if I've changed my mind, Doris?" "Too late now, kid," she told him. "The invitations are ordered."

We were married October fifth that year. And since then there have been good years, and bad years, but we've weathered it all together because we're a team. Teamwork is very important to a long and happy marriage. We'll be celebrating our forty-seventh wedding anniversary in October 2010. For the record, I wouldn't take back or change a moment of those years.

Born in Manhattan, **Bertrice Small** is the author of forty-nine novels. A *New York Times, Publishers Weekly, USA Today,* and *L.A. Times* bestselling author, she is the recipient of numerous awards including Career Achievement for Historical Romance; Career Achievement for Historical Fantasy. She was awarded a Lifetime Achievement Award by *Romantic Times* for her contributions to the Historical Romance genre. She was named by *Romantic Times,* along with her friends Jennifer Blake, Roberta Gellis, and Janelle Taylor, as a Pioneer of Romance. Please view her website at www.bertricesmall.com.

Amanda Scott
Then, Now, and Always

"I've got another cousin," my ex-neighbor Janie said when she telephoned. "'This one is taller, better looking, and funnier. He's my favorite cousin, and he wants a date, so you should go out with him. Here he is. Talk to him."

His version of the call goes something like this: "Janie said she knew this girl with a great personality—meaning she's probably plug-ugly and hard up for dates—who had gone out a few weeks before with Bill (his younger brother). I'd really like her, Janie said. She's dialing the phone as she tells me this, then she's telling you all that rot about being better looking and all, and then she says 'Here he is,' and hands me the damn phone."

It was the Saturday after Thanksgiving.

He asked if I'd like to have dinner some place in Monterey, and I agreed. His brother had been nice, both of them were Air Force officers, his brother had left the next day for foreign parts, and I figured he would do likewise. No harm, no foul . . . and dinner.

I was still date-shy after the death two years before of a guy I loved with all my heart., but I wasn't being a hermit and Terry sounded safe.

I was teaching second grade and living in a small apartment

behind my mother's house. My younger brother was in his junior year of high school and insisted that he would let me know when "the guy" arrived, and thereby get a good look at him first.

His verdict: "He's definitely taller."

I'm five foot three. When I walked into Mom's living room, Terry stood up, and it seemed to me that he just kept getting taller and taller. He's six foot four.

We talked nonstop from the minute we met, over dinner at the Sardine Factory, drinks at the Hyatt, driving to and from. The next night he called and asked if I'd go out again. I said I had to teach the next day and should put in some prep time. He said, "We won't stay out late."

We went for a drink and sat and talked. At some point, I said, "Do you remember the other day when we were talking about. . . ."

He chuckled. He said, "I only met you yesterday."

I felt as if I'd known him and talked with him all my life.

We had triple scoop ice cream cones at Baskin Robbins the next night, and went out together the next three nights (six dates in all). Then he flew back to Hawaii, where he was stationed. I couldn't go with him to the airport, because I had to teach. He was annoyed, but he sent me a big bunch of yellow rosebuds in a brandy snifter.

I'm a Leo, he's a Pisces. I'd explained that Leos tend to be a little royal. He addressed the flowers to "the Queen."

I wrote him a thank-you note. Mom raised me that way.

He replied with a long letter, and called a couple of days later. He'd managed to get the use of a MARS line, which meant that we could talk for free until someone with a higher priority (meaning anyone) wanted it. Then we'd be cut off without warning.

He wrote nearly every day through December and January. So did I.

Four days before Valentine's Day, he came back to California, and my cousin flew me to San Francisco to meet him. That night, Terry put a ring on my finger. He hadn't asked, hadn't ever even discussed the possibility of marriage, although heaven knows we'd talked about everything else under the sun. But he'd taken the chance that I'd say yes, picked out the diamond and the ring design, and had it made. He'd intended to give it to me on Valentine's Day, but he said he couldn't wait.

We married the day after school got out.

Meeting him was like finding the missing part of my soul. It still feels that way, as if we just fit together. It's decades later, and my heart still beats faster whenever I hear the garage door go up and know that he's come home.

As blind dates go, I'd say ours was a winner.

USA Today bestselling author and Romance Writers of America RITA Award winner, **Amanda Scott** is the author of more than fifty-five romances, nearly all of which are set in Scotland, England, and Wales. She lives in Northern California with her sweetheart husband and a fierce, soccer-playing cat named Willy Magee. Please visit her website at www.amandascottauthor.com.

Jennifer Blake

A Romantic Dreamer

Marrying at a young age is something of a tradition among the women in my family. We mature early, as is typical of subtropical climates such as the Deep South, but some unknown factor in our genes, pheromones, personalities, or appearance seems to make men want to have us around forever. My great-grandmother was married at sixteen, my grandmother at seventeen, and my mother at fifteen. I was also married at fifteen, my two daughters at ages sixteen and eighteen, and my granddaughter at eighteen. Despite these youthful weddings, the men we marry have seldom been the only ones to propose.

I met my husband when I was thirteen and he was seventeen. I was going out with his close friend at the time, so he was reluctant to make an obvious move. Instead, he wrote a series of anonymous poems, sending them over the next few months. In them were word plays on my name, touching images of how I appeared to him, and descriptions of his constant feelings and fantasies of how I might fit into his life.

I was your typical romantic dreamer even then. How was I to resist such an approach?

I soon guessed the identity of my poet, and we met again after a few weeks. By that time, I had broken off with his friend. We dated for over a year then became engaged shortly after my fifteenth birthday. The wedding was three months later. That was more than fifty years ago—but I still have those poems and his love.

Photo by Florian Kucheran

Jennifer Blake—Jennifer is a "pioneer of the romance genre" and an "icon of the romance industry." A *New York Times* and international bestselling author, she is a charter member of Romance Writers of America, a member of the RWA Hall of Fame. She received the RWA Lifetime Achievement RITA, and many other awards and honors. She has written more than sixty books with translations in twenty languages and more than 30 million copies in print worldwide. Jennifer lives in Louisiana with her husband, and a Shihtzu and a Maltese-poodle mix. Visit her website at www.jenniferblake.com.

Jo Ann Ferguson

Some (Less Than) Enchanted Evening

If a college friend hadn't had a huge fight with her boyfriend, I never would've met my husband Bill. My friend decided she really needed to see who else might be available in the dating pool. I wasn't seeing anyone seriously, so she tapped me to go with her on her big adventure. When she saw a notice for a party at a frat house on Friday night, she began trying to persuade me to go with her.

It took a lot of coaxing because I hated frat parties—too much beer, too much noise, too many guys trying to out-do each other. On the other hand, my friend had lent me her typewriter after I'd used up the last ribbon on mine while working on my first novel. That's a good friend, so I agreed we'd go to the frat party, have a few laughs, and then come home.

Friday night, we're set to go, looking good and excited about doing something so silly. The car was supposed to pick us up in ten minutes. Her phone rang. Guess who? Yes, it was her boyfriend, wanting to get together to talk things out. Did I mind if she canceled? Well, I did, but I'd worn out a couple of her typewriter's keys (which I hadn't mentioned to her yet), so I said I didn't mind.

The car was pulling up outside, and a bunch of giggly freshmen girls (do they make any other kind?) were agog with anticipation. When I, the lone non-frosh, got swept up, I went along. I decided to go, come home, and have a few laughs with my friends about me being at a frat party.

The frat party was everything I'd expected—and my expectations were low. I had to wait for the car to return after picking up more girls before I could get a ride back. Finally it came back. As I put down my untouched beer, I turned to thank the brother who'd driven us over, and it happened.

Across the crowded basement room with its beer-sticky floor, my gaze focused on a guy behind the bar. I always grin when I get to this part because if I put it in a novel, my editor would make me rewrite it. Yet as I looked across that crowded room, I knew he was the man I would marry. I didn't know him. I hadn't talked to him. He might have been a creep or boring or already married.

But I knew.

I went over, picked up another beer I wouldn't drink, and smiled at my future husband. He smiled back. A few minutes later, he came over to tell me his name was Bill and to ask me what I thought about the biggest issue on campus—demonstrations about food in the cafeterias. We started talking and laughing, and we kept talking and laughing all evening. We had more in common than we'd guessed. His roommate had dated one of my friends, and he'd worked backstage while I was on stage for Winter Carnival skits. But we'd never met. He took me home, kissed me good night (very nice!) and said he'd call later in the week.

I guess he might have, but I didn't get to find out. Monday night, my sorority decided to have a mixer the next night, and the sisters were supposed to bring dates. With my friend (now back with her boyfriend) and my roommate for moral support, I called Bill. I was less than calm, but he said yes. I hung up. The phone rang. It was my sorority sister saying the party had to be canceled. Now I had to call him back and "uninvite" him. He still claims there never really was a party, but he asked me out for the next night anyhow.

This year, we'll be celebrating thirty-five years of marriage. We still laugh a lot, and neither of us can believe that I actually went to that party or that we hadn't met before. But I guess it was fate, and we both had to be in that time and place for that evening that turned into an enchanted one.

Award-winning and bestselling author **Jo Ann Ferguson** is a past national president of Romance Writers of America. She has had more than ninety titles published under her name and as Jocelyn Kelly and Jo Ann Brown. They've been translated into almost a dozen languages and sold on every continent except Antarctica. Please visit her website at www.joannferguson.com.

Michele Ann Young

A Knight on a White Steed

It was the first time I'd hung out with some of the local teens in the bus shelter on the main road not far from our house. I'd been lured there by my sister, who thought I should meet people. Did I mention I grew up in England? We'd lived on the housing estate for three years, but I since travelled back to our old neighborhood for school. I didn't know any of the local kids.

So there we were, four girls in our pencil thin miniskirts and high heels hanging out in the dark at the bus stop. Could it get any more pathetic? A motorcycle drew up alongside us. It was the most beautiful bike I had ever seen in my life. White. It had what I later learned was called a dustbin fairing encasing the front of the bike. It looked like a rocket. The rider had dark hair, angular cheekbones, and a cheeky smile. My heart tumbled over.

"It's one of the Young boys," my sister said. "There are five of them."

Pulling off his gauntlets, he kicked the stand into place. "Wot's up." He was just so darned sexy I couldn't quite get my breath.

"Not much," I said.

He grinned at the group then his gaze honed in on me. "Want to go for a ride?"

You bet I did. Still, I had to play it cool. I shrugged. "All right."

"Hop on, then, love."

I hiked up my skirt, stepped on the footrest and perched behind him. My hands encountered solidly muscled shoulders encased in black leather. (Here I must issue a warning. In those days, helmets were not required, but I would never recommend riding without one, even though I did that night.)

"Put your arms around my waist and hold on." So I did and we roared off down the road.

Magic happened on that ride in the dark countryside with the wind whipping my long hair around my face and the bike leaning into the corners while I clung to the lithe body in front of me. And when we stopped on a nearby heath to talk, I discovered my knight in black leather on his white steed had a wonderfully wicked sense of humor and a faithful heart.

I've been putting my arms around his waist and holding on for the past thirty-five years. It really was love at first sight. And though I tease him sometimes and say it was the bike I fell for, I know it was really that cheeky smile.

Born in England and now living in Canada, **Michele Ann Young** has a husband, two lovely daughters, and a Maltese terrier called Teaser. After a successful career in business, her love of the past and the stories in her head led her to writing romances for several publishers as Michele Ann Young and for Harlequin as Ann Lethbridge. She loves the British Georgian and the Regency era. You will find her books under both names in bookstores, as well as on line. Visit her at www.annlethbridge.com or www.regencyramble.blogspot.com.

Nicola Cornick

Best Mistake I Ever Made

I was five years old when my parents divorced. I didn't see my father much after that; he hung around for a while but gradually he came to visit less and less. The last time I saw him I was about eleven years old and he gave me a piece of advice. "Never get married," he said. "It's a big mistake." I took his advice to heart. I couldn't imagine ever trusting anyone enough to love them wholeheartedly, let alone marry them, and I was determined that if I ever did get married I would be old—at least thirty-five.

Fate wasn't listening though. In my second year at London University, when I was nineteen, I met Andrew. I was at a party and I suddenly had the feeling that someone was watching me. I turned around and we had one of those classic eyes across a crowded room moments. I knew in an instant that he was The One and hot on the heels of that thought came another—that this was too big and too important and too scary, and that I was too young to handle it because at the back of my mind was the image of my father walking away forever, and I never wanted that to happen to me again.

Andrew and I became friends and it was great. We would talk about everything under the sun, staying up until three in the morning just chatting. We shared a taste in music and an interest in hiking and in nature and wildlife. When we left college we stayed friends and wrote long letters to each other. He was always there for me. I knew that he liked me and that he was waiting, giving me time. It felt reassuring to have him in my life but it was too scary to make a commitment to turn our friendship into something else, something romantic.

After four years Andrew rang me and told me that he couldn't wait for me any longer and that it was time for him to try to find someone else. I can still remember how I felt after I put the phone down. I was shocked and baffled, as though I had lost something infinitely precious that I hadn't really valued until it was too late. I remember thinking: "He can't find someone else. He belongs to me." I knew I loved him and that I had taken his love for granted.

I was frightened. I knew that if I wanted Andrew I had to take the risk. Suddenly I realized that I would never feel more grown up than I did now, that it was nothing to do with age and everything to do with having faith. We started to date and after three months we got engaged. Six months after that we were married.

I rang my father up to give him the news when Andrew and I got engaged. He said: "You're too young. You're making a mistake." This time I said: "No, I'm not. It's not about age. It's about having faith in love."

Photo by Andrew Cornick

Nicola Cornick studied history at London University and Ruskin College, Oxford. She writes historical romance for Harlequin HQN Books in the United States and MIRA Books U.K. She is also an historian and a double nominee for both the Romantic Novelists' Association Romance Prize and the Romance Writers of America RITA award. Nicola has been described by *Publisher's Weekly* as "a rising star of the Regency genre." Her website is www.nicolacornick.co.uk.

Kasey Michaels
I Want Him

So it was a Friday night and I had to work late and my girlfriend insisted I meet her afterward at a local teen hangout where a bored janitor spun records and some people danced and everyone sized each other up and mostly stuck with who they came with—the girls at one end of the floor, the boys congregating at the other.

And then there he was, standing at the entrance to the place, dressed in tight black dress slacks, crisp white dress shirt open at the collar, early '60s skinny black tie loosened at his neck, his silk black patterned vest unbuttoned. In a room filled with guys in jeans and T-shirts, I mean, you just couldn't miss him.

His black hair was thick and sort of high, combed back from his forehead, and his eyes were greener than green (okay, so I found out that last part later). He looked like a young Ricky Nelson . . . and if you've never seen photos of a young Ricky Nelson, Google him. Trust me. This was not a bad thing!

I was tired, I had been bored; I was feeling . . . restless. I nudged my girlfriend and then shamelessly pointed across the room, saying, "I want him."

To which my girlfriend rolled her eyes and responded, "Him?

That's Mike. He's the guy I've been trying to set you up with for a year, but you said you didn't want a blind date."

Duh.

My friend introduced us. After that, things are kind of blurry. We danced; I remember that. We danced every dance. He drove home behind me, to make sure I got there safely (Ah, come on—what wasn't to like about this guy!). He phoned me every night and we talked for hours; about what, I have no idea.

The next Friday night we went to the movies (Jackie Gleason, in *Gigot*). Mike took my hand in the dark theater, my entire world shifted on its axis, and I surprised myself by not throwing up in the popcorn cup.

We saw each other every night the following week, and he'd kiss me goodnight at my door, get halfway across the lawn to his car, turn around and come back, kiss me again. Sometimes that ritual repeated itself a half dozen times a night. Then he'd drive home and call me and we'd, yes, talk for hours. I still don't remember what we talked about.

The following Friday (we're measuring this in Fridays . . .) he proposed. Well, sort of proposed. He said he cared for me, "a lot." I said you care for movies, and dogs, and baseball teams—you don't care for a person (I was pretty gutsy at nineteen . . .). Poor guy. The next thing he knew he was telling me he loved me, and the next thing I knew I was asking, "Does that mean you want to marry me?" And the next thing he knew, he was saying yes, he did.

Met in January, engaged in April, married in June. We both were still only nineteen (translation: young and dumb).

You're now asking yourself: Did she ever use any of this in one of her books? The answer is: Oh yeah! You don't write romance novels if you don't believe in romance.

Do I believe in love at first sight? Maybe. I know I believe in instant attraction, I believe in your heart knowing something long before your mind and even your common sense begin to catch up.

Do I believe in happy endings? No, I don't.

What begins in giddiness and passion for each other can end just as swiftly if you don't work at keeping the love alive, and believe in sticking together when times get rough and then get even rougher. Hell, I wrote a book about it (. . . *Or You Can Let Him Go;* Kathryn Seidick), about what life is like when your young child is suddenly faced with a life-threatening illness, in our son's case, renal failure and transplant, twice in six years.

You marry with stars in your eyes, we all do. Sometimes we're lucky, sometimes we're not. You have to bury your premature son. You pace the floor during your husband's emergency surgery because his aorta is about to burst. You deal with cancer. You juggle kids, and aging parents, and bills—because this is real life. We all live it.

Nobody promised any of us a rose garden, right? So there has to be more than love, passion. There has to be commitment on every level, and that's not easy sometimes, it's not fun, it's not what we all thought as we blithely recited "for richer, for poorer, in sickness and in health" and the rest of that stuff.

So nearly forty-eight years after that silly young girl pointed across a room and imperiously declared: "I want him," five children and seven grandsons later, why is the memory of that first night still not only clear to me, but also so important? That's easy to answer. You need to remember the love, always remember the love, even when Real Life gives it to you on the chin. It's still the love that comes first, the love that endures, the love that gets you through.

Bestselling author, **Kasey Michaels** has written more than 110 books. She is a recipient of a RITA Award, among other honors, and is a past president of Novelists, Inc. A non-fiction work, . . . *Or You Can Let Him Go*, details the story of her eldest son's first kidney transplant. Reach Kasey at www.kaseymichaels.com.

Eloisa James
How I Found True Love

I grew up on a farm in rural Minnesota. But my father, Robert Bly, was no farmer. He was a long-haired, serape-wearing poet of the 1960s, interested in antiwar marches, not soybeans. He was jailed for leading protests against the Vietnam War, won the American Book Award for Poetry, and pulled us out of school to live in England, France, and Norway for a year at a time. He was reckless with money, not that there was much. His view of the relative worth of poetry versus designer clothing was never a question.

Naturally, I went to college determined to find my father's opposite, get a high-paying job, and wear designer clothing every day. I met the very man in my first year at Harvard: a would-be banker who drove a convertible and knew a lot about oriental rugs. His mother was horrified by my braless state; we were perfect for each other. We stayed together for ten years.

When I think about finding true love, I see it as a journey that includes the roadblock of one's parents. When I finally broke up with my banker, he pointed out that I didn't respect him. That was true: in essence, I had chosen him for precisely that reason.

My friends started setting me up on blind dates. I went out with a future doctor, and a future lawyer. Ho-hum. Finally, I found myself in the company of a Florentine with a ravishing accent, wild black hair to his shoulders, and a degree in medieval Italian literature. He was exotic and entirely delicious. After this little fling, I told myself, I'll settle down and find a husband.

That Italian asked me to marry him when we were living in Princeton, where he was teaching at the university. We went for a walk along their beautiful river, and climbed out to sit on a fallen tree draped over the river. He asked the question and pulled me into his arms . . . I promptly dropped my keys into the water!

How to get them back? He had to teach in a few hours and couldn't show up in class wet to his waist. But since he was (of course) a true knight in shining armor, he took off his pants and climbed into the water and mud to get my keys back. I was laughing so hard that I almost fell off the log myself. He still remembers being terrified that one of his students would come up the river path and see him in his boxer shorts (he was a very young professor then, and anxious about his dignity).

The night before my wedding, my father leapt to his feet with an improvised poem. My former banker gave a measured, prepared toast. Finally, my husband came to his feet with a creative, poetic, and ebullient thank you.

The next day, I married a man exactly like my father. Take away the exotic accent, and I had found the solid core I learned at home: an understanding of the fundamental irrelevance of a life bounded by materialistic concerns, together with deep creativity and a passion for literature.

My Italian husband is a knight, a cavalier—the perfect consort for a romance author. That wasn't how I saw him at first, which is why I love novels about bad boys who turn into wonderful husbands. I'm tremendously lucky, and I like to make sure that my heroines are just as lucky as I am!

People magazine raved of **Eloisa James**'s writing that "romance writing does not get much better than this." A *New York Times* bestseller many times over, Eloisa is also a Shakespeare professor. She's the mother of two children and, in a delicious irony for a romance writer, is married to an Italian knight. Her website is www.eloisajames.com.

Secret Key #3

Inspiration

My stock in trade is thinking about what it means to be in love. Lasting love. The love we all profess to desire. How does one measure it? Or define it? Certainly time isn't a good indicator of love. I've witnessed couples who have lived together for years, marry, and then split. There are those who have the right jobs, the right security, the right religion, or voting record, and it isn't enough. Meanwhile, two sailors without much to their names stumble upon each other and the love lasts.

Sometimes souls collide; sometimes they willingly slip together; sometimes they linger only for a moment before moving on to love again. I may not understand how love is mastered, but I do know it is worth the risk.

–Cathy Maxwell

Pamela Morsi

Lightning Strikes Twice

I almost didn't go. It was a blind date and I hadn't been impressed over the phone. But at the last minute, I decided to show up at the place we'd agreed upon.

I spotted him immediately, sitting at the bar. He was dressed, as he said he would be, in a pinstripe suit with a carnation in his lapel. I was wearing a T-shirt and jeans.

I walked right up to him.

"Hi, I'm Pam."

He looked up at me. Those big, dark eyes that I now see in the faces of my son and my daughter, widened.

"I never expected you to be so beautiful," he said.

I may have fallen in love with him that night. Or maybe I just realized how easy falling for him was going to be. I do remember talking to my mom on the phone the next day and warning her that I thought this one was special.

And he was. We were best friends, confidants, lovers for the next twenty years. He was solid, hardworking, and responsible. He had great confidence in me as a mom and as a professional woman. And when I confessed my desire to become a writer, he encouraged me. More than that, he spent hours with a calculator and pencil doing the financial planning necessary for me to take on such a risky career move.

He had a wonderful deep voice, a very dry wit, and a deep love of his family, his friends, his fellow man. When he died after a long and exhausting illness, I felt both cheated out of our future together and grateful for the years we had.

Perhaps the most honest thing to admit is that widowhood truly didn't suit me. After the first year of shock and numbness, I realized that I had almost no role model to emulate. My parents and both sets of grandparents had happy, long marriages. And when one died, the other followed within a very short time.

At age forty-five and in perfect health, it seemed as if, unless I stepped in front of a bus, I was going to have to keep on living. And I wasn't all that keen on doing it alone. But I wasn't sure there were any other options.

I had often secretly ascribed to the "one true love" school of romance and marriage. Of course it's not logical that there would only be one. The human race couldn't have survived if every person had to find just that one right person. But logic and attitudes about love rarely go together.

Also, I'm a special needs mom. And I was honest enough with myself to realize that didn't enhance my attractiveness in the marriage mart. Men like women with little or no emotional baggage. Emotional baggage is the definition of a special needs mom.

Add to that a bit of what I call the Coretta Scott King syndrome. When a woman has been married to someone really amazing, how could she ever settle for somebody just ordinary? And ordinary is what you're bound to find. Lightning never strikes the same place twice.

I was not alone in my reticence. When I mentioned to my sister that I was thinking of dating she warned me that there were no decent guys to be had. "I know what's out there and I just don't want you to be hurt," she said.

My son was equally discouraging. "He wants you to be happy," my daughter-in-law related on his behalf. "He'd just prefer that you be happy alone."

So after a year of being in shock and grief, and a year of weighing my options, at the beginning of year three of my life as a widow, I decided that rather than searching for true love, I'd just try to find somebody to go with me to the movies.

I have to admit here that I am an unstoppable movie buff. Yes, there have been periods that I missed completely, like the years my hometown theater closed and the frantic decade of juggling career, illness, and kids. But for most of my life I've just refused to pass up the blockbuster flicks, the off-beat indies, even the subtitled foreign films. There is almost nothing I like better than the darkness of the room with no interruptions and a great story laid out to watch. Going to the movies alone is okay. But going with someone else is always better.

Fairy tale wisdom suggests that a woman must kiss a lot of frogs to find a prince. I would paraphrase that I had to eat a lot of popcorn to find a movie companion.

I met some great guys and had a lot of nice nights out. The "bad dates" could be totaled up on one hand. Then in May of 1999 I met Bill.

At the time I was way too busy and missing a lot of great films. My career was careening, my kids were creating havoc, and I was getting prepared to go to the hospital for surgery. I didn't have time for so much as a Documentary Short! But fate seems to have its own timetable.

Bill walked into my life with a hat and a toothy grin. He was so perfect for me, I couldn't believe he was true. The first time I invited him to my house, he found a print of his favorite painting hanging on my kitchen wall. We were interested in the same things, laughed at all the same jokes. He could be there when I needed him, but left me alone when I needed time for myself. He is smart and focused and endlessly curious. He'd grown up in the world of science and brought a new perspective to everything I researched.

He dove into the world of disabled, becoming a Special Olympics coach. He hit it off with my aging parents, who liked him immediately. His kids liked my kids and vice versa.

I resisted as long as I could. Even when I said, "I love you," I immediately took it back. But I just couldn't keep him at a distance.

Sometimes movies are not enough. Sometimes you just have to walk into the sunset. And sometimes lightning strikes the same place twice.

Pamela Morsi is a bestselling, award-winning novelist who finds humor in everyday life and honor in ordinary people. She lives in San Antonio, Texas, with her husband and daughter. Please visit her website at www.pamelamorsi.com.

Kate Austin

Smacked by Fate

It isn't easy being smacked in the face by fate, but it's definitely interesting.

But to tell this story, I have to tell you things about myself that only my best friends know. I was fifty-one years old. I'd been single pretty much all of my grown-up life with the exception of a very short—and foolish—marriage and one long-term relationship for a total of eight years. You can do the math.

Here's the key to everything that follows: I love being single. I'm a writer, so I love living by myself. And I love first dates the same way I love job interviews. I've never been to an interview when I didn't get the job; never been on a first date that didn't lead to a second. I love getting to know people. I love talking to strangers. So the last thing I wanted was a real relationship.

Here's where fate intervenes.

I was having a wonderful time. I was dating four or five men at a time and they lived all over North America, which meant I got to do a lot of traveling. I saw them for a few days in their city or in mine. I could be as solitary as I wanted most of the time and I was having the time of my life.

"I'm going to be single for the rest of my life," I said to my friends. "I love being single. I've finally figured out how my life was meant to be."

Smack.

I have a favorite restaurant, Don Francesco's, a lovely Italian restaurant in the heart of Vancouver. I've known Francesco for thirty years and his restaurant was my home away from home. I went there for my birthday, I took friends from out of town, I dropped in for a drink if I was having a bad day, or on my way home from shopping if I needed a bite to eat and a glass of wine. Everyone knew me and I knew all of them.

So when Saeed stopped by my table one night and asked me out, of course I said yes. Because one of the other things I had figured out was that saying yes rather than no made my life more interesting and exciting and satisfying.

I thought it was just another date with a very attractive man. He was handsome, he had beautiful amber eyes, he was beautifully dressed and groomed, and smelled great. He had a lovely accent and a body to die for.

Dinner was a bit awkward. English isn't his first language and I could tell he was uncomfortable. But I didn't mind sitting across the table from this beautiful man and, as always, I did most of the talking. We talked about our pasts and our families—he's the only boy and has six older sisters. We talked about food and wine and cars and sports and books and movies.

And we made another date for a walk on the beach. And then another. And another. I forgot all about my carefully laid plans for my life.

I can still remember the exact place and the exact moment

when he told me he loved me—a beautiful quiet street in the heart of Vancouver, surrounded by late spring flowers and glorious sunshine. We'd only been seeing each other for two or three weeks, but those weeks had been intense. I'm sorry to admit that I didn't say it back to him and I know he was hurt by that refusal. But I couldn't. I wasn't ready to give up the life I had just weeks earlier thought so perfect.

It took me another three weeks to admit that I'd already given up the life I'd boasted of to my friends and to tell him that I loved him. Oddly, I don't remember where we were when that happened.

For the next year, we saw each other two or three or four times a week. We walked on the beach. We went to the gym together and I saw—and enjoyed—that beautiful body stripped down. We went out to breakfast, lunch, and dinner. He met my family and friends. I met his. And not once in that year did I feel overwhelmed, unhappy, or uncomfortable about changing my perfect and solitary existence so completely.

But, as my friends will tell you, when I'm in, I'm in. And so, although it took a few months and a few late nights, I finally convinced Saeed that we should share living space. And we did. Almost exactly one year from the day we met, we finished painting his apartment and we moved in together. It hasn't always been easy—there were hundreds of decisions to make. How do we fit two households into one? Whose dishes? Whose phone number? Do we need more glasses? Where do we put the office?

As you can imagine, two Aries in one small apartment makes for some fiery battles but we've learned—mostly—how to deal with those. Because, really, none of them are important. What is important is that both of us know how lucky we are to have found each other at this stage of our lives. My life has changed completely and, although sometimes I might wish for a little more time to myself, I wouldn't give up what I have for anything.

So the moral to this story? Be careful. Be careful what you say and be careful that you don't get too complacent. Because fate will smack you down in a way you could never have anticipated. It might be wonderful, but it'll definitely be a shock.

Photo by Heather Armour

Kate Austin is a multi-published author of women's fiction. She has published eight books with Harlequin's and a novella, *Summertime Blues*, was included in the Summer Fever anthology published by Mills & Boon. Her short erotic fiction *Dreamer* is online now with Spice Briefs. She has a dozen short pieces of erotica online from Cobblestone Press under the name Josée Renard. For more information about Kate or Josée, visit her websites at www.KateAustin.ca or www.JoseeRenard.com.

Deb Stover

Our Hero

I often tell people it's no wonder I grew up to write romance novels, because I believe in heroes. I was raised by one, and I married one.

Like most nineteen-year-olds, I thought I knew everything. In 1976, while still living at home with my parents, working full-time, and trying to go to school part-time, a good friend insisted on introducing me to someone her fiancé worked with at McConnell Air Force Base. It would be a double date—a blind date. Oh, goodie. I was young, but not stupid. By nineteen, I'd suffered through a few blind dates.

To make matters worse, it was my date's twenty-first birthday. A young airman newly assigned to McConnell, he hadn't met many people, so he would celebrate his birthday with us. And how did we celebrate in 1976? By seeing *Young Frankenstein*, of course.

Dave Stover was tall, muscular, blond, blue-eyed, and extremely good-looking. In fact, he bore a remarkable resemblance to the young actor who played the role of Rolfe in *The Sound of Music*. After a few weeks I introduced him to my mother, and I asked her what she thought. She sighed and said, "I think he's a walking, living, breathing doll."

And so he was. . . .

We had a whirlwind courtship. There's no other way to describe it. We met in April, became engaged in May, and married in August. Many said it wouldn't last. After all, we were so young. We barely knew each other.

But we knew. . . .

On August 6, 1976, I married my Prince Charming. Our first year of marriage wasn't easy, as I became ill with serious blood clots in my leg that traveled to my lung just before our first anniversary. It was frightening, but we grew closer as we dealt with our trials.

When we started trying to have a family, we discovered my clotting problem was genetic, and that pregnancy complicated it. In fact, it was life threatening. I had to give myself injections every six hours throughout my pregnancies. Our twin daughters were born prematurely in 1980 and died shortly after their birth.

One month later, my mother-in-law died from cancer. It was a very bad time, but every day brought us closer; every trial made us stronger.

In December 1981, we were blessed with our beautiful, full-term baby girl, Barbi. It would be my last pregnancy, as my obstetrician told us another attempt was "paramount to a death wish."

We dedicated our lives to each other, and to spoiling our daughter. After four years, we looked into adoption, and took a workshop on special needs adoption. Three months later, we brought home Bonnie—a newborn with Down syndrome and congenital heart disease. She's now twenty-four and pure sunshine mixed with Missouri Mule.

Three years later, when I suggested we consider a multiracial child, Dave didn't even hesitate. So we brought home our son, Benjamin, who is too good looking for his own good. The girls follow him everywhere.

As I worked to publish my first novel, and raised our children, Dave worked at his career, completed his MBA, and we were forced to move around the country more than once. But he always supported my efforts, never suggested I stop trying to sell that first book, or ceased to be our children's greatest inspiration in all their endeavors.

In December 1999, the day before our oldest child's eighteenth birthday, Dave was diagnosed with stage III colon cancer. The next year was an endless stream of radiation, chemotherapy, surgeries, and stress. Finally, he was pronounced "in remission."

In the spring of 2001, still in remission, he accepted a promising position in Oregon. Filled with anticipation, we moved halfway across the country for a new beginning. Cancer free, a new career, a new home, a new life. I was contracted for my twelfth novel, our oldest child was on the high dean's list in college, and our younger two were doing well in school.

When Dave's cancer came out of remission in 2004, he had just returned from a trip with the United States Air Force Reserve. He fought his cancer with courage and love as he did everything else in his life, and he did it for us.

When, after months of treatments, it became clear his cancer was terminal, we planned the family's return to Colorado together. He asked me to take his ashes home to Colorado with his family.

The hardest thing I've ever done was to hold my hero's hand and let him go. I promised him I would take care of his family, and of myself. Because, being the hero he was, he would not let go, no matter how much pain he was in, until he was sure I would be okay.

David Allen Stover: Hero, Husband, Father, Friend . . .

April 21, 1955-May 14, 2005

We love you always.

Since publication of *Shades of Rose* in 1995, **Deb Stover** has received dozens of awards for her cross-genre fiction, including Pikes Peak Romance Writers' Author of the Year, a Career Achievement Award in 2004 from Romantic Times, and their Reviewer's Choice Award in 1999. Her twelfth novel, *The Gift*, was released in November 2009. For more information, please visit www.debstover.com.

Sabrina Jeffries
The Love of My Life

I met my husband Rene at a very unlikely place—my very first Mardi Gras in New Orleans. I'd gone there with friends from Tulane, my graduate school. My husband was with his friend Steve, who was dating a friend of a friend from Tulane. I'd met Steve earlier at a grad school party. Later, when I was out on the street alone, I happened to look around, eager for company, and I spotted Steve (he was hard to miss, since he was over six feet tall and dressed as Gandolf, wearing one of those high pointy hats). That's when he introduced me to Rene.

Rene was dressed as a jester, in full makeup and a costume (I was dressed as a harem girl). All I could see of his face was his beard. But we chatted for a while and discovered we had many of the same interests—costuming, ethnic food (actually, food of any kind), philosophy, books. . . . Since we both knew the woman throwing the grad school party, Rene asked if I would be interested in going to dinner if he got my phone number from her. I said sure.

At the time I didn't think it odd that he hadn't just asked for my number right out, but some time later I wondered about it. When I asked him to explain, he said he'd wanted to give me a chance to find out from our mutual friend if he was a decent guy before he called me to ask me out. He hadn't wanted to put me on the spot!

That is just a small illustration of how thoughtful and sensitive my lovely husband is. He bought me my first computer and printer before we were even married. (And whoever said that ladies shouldn't accept gifts from gentlemen never had a man buy her office equipment—be still, my heart!) He was the first person in my life to encourage me to write what I wanted. He gave me books on writing and watched our son without complaint when I spent one Saturday a month at my local writer's meeting.

That last thing was a bigger deal than anyone could realize, since our only son Nick was diagnosed with autism at a young age. Even there, my husband was my rock. HE was the one who insisted on getting a good diagnosis when I was in denial, who got up early to bathe and dress Nick for school after I stayed up late caring for him at night, who pushed for our move to North Carolina so we could gain better opportunities for our child. Even during the years when Nick was almost more than one person could handle, Rene was always ready to take over while I wrote books or attended writing conferences or did book signings.

Now that Nick is grown and doing extremely well in a job for disabled adults, I can look back and see how much my husband had to do with that. We've been married for twenty-six years, and he's always been the only man who really "gets" me—who's a true soul mate. So I can truthfully say, thank goodness for friends who hook you up with the love of your life!

Sabrina Jeffries is the award-winning author of thirty novels, four novellas, and three short stories, including the recent entry in her Hellions of Halstead Hall series, *A Hellion in Her Bed*. After earning her Ph.D., she chose writing over academics, and now her sexy and humorous historical romances routinely land on the *New York Times* and *USA Today* bestseller lists. She lives in Cary with her husband and son. Please visit her website at www.sabrinajeffries.com.

Gayle Callen

Finding Love in the Most Unlikely Place

I received my marriage proposal in a cemetery.

This may seem very unromantic, but let me explain. My husband, Jim, comes from a large family—he has six brothers and sisters younger than he is. When we met and began dating in college, his sister was two years old. Many of our dates involved him helping to take care of his family first, whether it was dropping his teenage sisters at the roller skating rink, or shopping at the grocery store and making a quick dinner for his brothers and sisters when his parents were out of town. Jim did all the cooking while I watched in amazement. The two year old and six year old climbed into my lap, talking nonstop.

Jim tolerated everything, even though my attention was not always on him. Within a month I knew I was head over heels in love. We shared the same sense of humor, the same outlook on life and having children, a great physical attraction, yet we were different enough to make things interesting.

When we decided to get married, we were very young. I always tell my children we were the lucky ones, since we didn't have a lot, but we loved each other. I didn't expect a ring or a house, but strange quirks of fate began to happen. His grandfather just happened to have a fully furnished, unoccupied house; the church and reception hall suddenly had cancellations for the date we wanted.

On the day we were to announce our engagement to his brothers and sisters at a family dinner, Jim picked me up at my dorm. To my surprise, he turned into the old, scenic cemetery behind campus. It was the kind of place meant to be a peaceful park, where students laid in the sun to study. He told me that between his crazy house and my dorm, he couldn't find any privacy at all. And since I'm from a family of funeral directors, I've never had a problem with cemeteries.

But I still didn't know why he needed privacy until he brought out the tiny box. I was stunned, for I'd never expected it. And then he explained the history of the ring. His biological father had died when he was a year old, and this had been the ring he'd given to Jim's mother. She'd remarried when Jim was four, saving this ring for Jim, although he'd never known.

He put the ring on my finger, and it meant more than just a promise between us. It had a history of love, one that we could continue.

USA Today bestselling author **Gayle Callen** writes historical romances for Avon Books. Her most recent novel, *A Most Scandalous Engagement,* was published in December 2010. Gayle's novels have won the Holt Medallion, Laurel Wreath Award, and Reader's Choice Awards. Her books have been translated into more than eight different languages. Gayle resides in central New York with her husband and three children. Please visit her website at www.gaylecallen.com.

Mary Jo Putney

Love: In Sickness and in Health

How can a couple keep things romantic? Well, a near death experience can help.

Most of us are so busy all the time that the little things in life—the moments of connection with our nearest and dearest—can easily get lost in the rush. I'm lucky that as a full-time writer, my life is not as complicated and busy as most, but even so, too often the fun things get postponed in favor of what seems more urgent.

John and I have always had a romantic streak. One might even say silly and sentimental, since we enjoy stuffed animals and greeting cards of kittens and the like.

But with both of us busy with our careers, there wasn't always enough time to just enjoy each other. Some weekends, I'd be flying home from a conference and know that John was somewhere else in the airport, flying off for a teaching or consulting gig.

Then John suffered a major stroke at age fifty. If I hadn't been in the next room to call for help, very likely he would have died. (Thank God for 911 and the EMTs who respond. No kidding.)

Much later, John reported that as he lay half paralyzed on a bed, unable to sit up or eat without help, and his breathing needed some aid, too, what he most regretted was that we hadn't made more trips to B&Bs. Maybe now he would never be able to do that again.

We both love bed and breakfast inns because each is unique and they are always labors of love on the part of the hosts. Now and then we would go off into the country and stay in a nice B&B, but not that often. There would be time for such things later.

We all know that time isn't infinite, but that knowledge doesn't turn visceral until disaster strikes. Then we become aware all the way down to our DNA that every minute really does count. John came home in a wheelchair, not sure if he'd ever walk again, and with a lot of his natural joie de vivre extinguished.

A few months later, for his birthday, I gave him two handmade certificates for B&B stays. By then, he was walking a little, able to climb a few steps, but even so, it was a challenge to find B&Bs that he could access.

I managed. So did he. (There is nothing like having a loved one in a wheelchair to make a person appreciate handicapped access, and which businesses make an effort and which don't.)

Several years have passed and John is much more mobile now, and we're both a whole lot better at taking the time to enjoy each other. There are the trips—since his stroke we've been to Alaska, the Caribbean, South Africa, Portugal, Australia, and New Zealand, among other places.

But even more important are the moments. Reading the Sunday paper together while we sip coffee and interrupt each other with choice bits of news. Watching the cats chase a laser dot. (John is world class at running those kitties around.)

Sometimes work gets put aside to go out for lunch at a nice little place by the bay. I make sure I pick up the special cookies I know he likes. We send each other silly e-mails, sometimes when we're sitting in adjacent chairs with our laptops. Conferences might be left early so as to get home in time to enjoy a meal together.

Romance is in the special moments when you remember why you love this person. Don't waste a single precious instant.

A *New York Times* bestselling author, **Mary Jo Putney** was born in upstate New York with a reading addiction, a condition with no known cure. Her entire writing career is an accidental byproduct of buying a computer for other purposes. Most of her books contain history, romance, and cats. Please visit her website at www.maryjoputney.com.

Cathy Maxwell

The Most Dangerous Thing

The most dangerous thing I've done in my life is marry a man I'd known for only a month.

Max and I met while we were both serving in the Navy. I didn't like him at first. Of course, you knew that. Many of the best marriages start off with that admission. I had a plan for my life. A career. And then this big Irish-American with a supersized personality blew all those plans away.

You wonder if, after only a month of courting, did I know him well enough to marry?

Absolutely not. But he liked to laugh, had a good family, made me feel safe, and we could talk.

The decision to wed was abrupt. We didn't bother to ask parental permission. I flew home with him at my side, no word of warning to my parents that I was seriously dating, and announced without preamble that we would be married.

One priest refused to marry us because of the suddenness of our desires. We found another priest. That simple. We were confident in what we were doing, ignored those around us that shook their heads with doubt or predicted doom, . . . and for the next twenty-five years forged one helluva partnership. Not even death dims my love for him.

The other day, my youngest informed me she is getting married—to a guy she's known for only a month. If she'd hit me over the head with a baseball bat my reaction would have been the same. The adage "what goes around comes around" has never rung truer.

I didn't know this man. I'd only met him for all of three minutes of introductions and then I'd been called away to another part of the country for a month and in that time, she fell in love.

She'd phone. She thought she was keeping me apprised of the relationship. The first week, she told me she'd found "the one." The second week, she confessed if he asked, she'd marry him. I was, surprisingly, pretty smug in my belief that she wouldn't just up and get engaged. After all, she needed my approval and discerning time and all the other cautions I'd offered over the years (and over that month of phone calls).

Three and a half weeks after she met him, he offered a ring and she said yes. No hesitation, no doubts, no worries . . . no calling her mother to ask permission?

Their wedding is a few months away. They are different from Max and me since they'll actually be in the same city while making those wedding plans.

My friends do the worrying. So soon, too soon, they say, but I disagree.

You see, my stock in trade is thinking about what it means to be in love. Lasting love. The love we all profess to desire. How does one measure it? Or define it?

Certainly time isn't a good indicator of love. I've witnessed couples who have lived together for years, marry, and then split.

Or be married for decades and, in the sunset of their lives when all battles should have been settled, head for divorce court. There are those who have the right jobs, the right security, the right religion or voting record, and it isn't enough.

Meanwhile, two sailors without much to their names stumble upon each other and the love lasts.

Oh, I don't think one should jump in and marry someone cruel or whacky or, even worse, selfish. There should be a fear of that. I do believe in discernment, especially for my children—but I'm beginning to know this man who holds my daughter's heart in his hands and I like him. He's kind. He knows how to laugh. He has a good family. His eyes light up with enthusiasm for life and for her. Both of them seem equally determined to make their marriage work.

Are those qualities predictors of success? I hope so.

Sometimes souls collide; sometimes they willingly slip together; sometimes they linger only for a moment before moving on to love again. I may not understand how love is mastered, but I do know it is worth the risk.

So I pray that someday, I will overhear my daughter admit, "The most dangerous thing I've done in my life is marry a man I'd known only a month." May she make the boast with pride and with the success of one who loves well.

Photo by Anthony Rumley

Cathy Maxwell is the *New York Times* and *USA Today* bestselling author of more than twenty historical romance novels. She never minds spending hours in front of her computer pondering the question, "Why do people fall in love?" To her, it remains the great mystery of life and the secret to happiness. To discover more about Cathy and her books, visit www.cathymaxwell.com.

Secret Key #4

Opposites Attract

Dissing your beloved to others is a step down the slippery slope toward contempt, and no relationship can thrive with even a speck of contempt in it. Accept and respect your partner for who he or she is. That acceptance is a powerful motivator for trust, and a long life together is all about making yourself vulnerable to your partner, not waiting for it to be done for you first. Doing so requires courage, but that courage will be rewarded a thousandfold. A long love affair needs a special, private, safe place to grow and blossom. Creating that space is, I believe with all my heart, both the joy and the most sacred duty of a marriage.

–Jean Brashear

Jean Brashear

Celebrate Your Differences

My beloved and I have been married forty years now and, quite seriously, we're more in love than ever. It's not the original infatuation; it's deeper and richer, more powerful for having endured through life's roller coaster. Raising children, handling family crises, financial ups and downs . . . all of these tested two kids who came together out of an inexplicable resonance and more than a little heat. We had no game plan, no money, no college degrees, no family pedigrees to fall back on.

We only had love, and our understanding of that was admittedly fuzzy. We certainly came to the enterprise from differing points of view. Though I'd never read a romance novel back then, I'm a bone-deep romantic. He's a former Marine and Mr. Pragmatic. I'm a vegetarian; he's a diehard carnivore. We're on opposite sides of many an issue, and we're both hardheaded as an old billy goat.

So how are we still together forty years later, much less having the best time of our lives? It's not that we haven't been tested—we have. So what did we do that got us here, still thrilled to wake up together each day?

Well, first of all, we refused to give up; we didn't run when things got dicey. Life is hard; marriage is a challenge. We didn't stake out our territory and insist on 50/50—life (and love) don't work that way. Sometimes it's 90/10, and who's giving the 90 changes constantly. Another critical factor is that we make each other a priority (never forget to date your spouse!) even when families and work and the world in general keep jockeying for attention. Put each other first—when the kids are grown, if you've focused everything on them, you'll find yourself married to a stranger. Ditto with your career. Stay in touch. And flirt!

Respect is also a crucial ingredient in a happy marriage—we don't complain about our spouses to our friends; we work it out between us. Dissing your beloved to others is a step down the slippery slope toward contempt, and no relationship can thrive with even a speck of contempt in it.

Another important attribute of the man I love and, I hope of me, too: he not only gave me room to grow but encouraged me to do so. There's an old saw that women marry men hoping to change them, and men marry women hoping they'll never change . . . and neither dynamic works in the long term. My life as a published author is a perfect example—when writing was only a crazy dream for me, he believed. He not only encouraged me but went out of his way to do so, and he never lost faith, however often I did, that I would make it. No one is more proud of my successes, and his continuing faith and constant delight are my refuge through the rough spots that are an inevitable part of the world of publishing.

People thought the odds were against us making it, much less making anything of ourselves, yet he's a college graduate and prominent in his field and in our community. He's a driving force in the lives of others. He says I'm his joy and his sunshine. Yes, we had to rub a lot of rough edges off the differences between us, but we've come through all that as each other's best friend. We grew up together, and we're not finished growing. There's still so much that each of us wants to do, and while the other may not be in the least interested in that activity (you won't find me in the boonies hunting with him or him exploring art galleries in the city with me) we're both intensely interested in each other and respect what leads each of us down diverse paths.

Because in the end, we come back to our shared world, our life and our love the richer for it. Celebrate your differences. Accept and respect your partner for who he or she is. That acceptance is a powerful motivator for trust, and a long life together is all about making yourself vulnerable to your partner, not waiting for it to be done for you first. Doing so requires courage, but that courage will be rewarded a thousandfold.

A long love affair needs a special, private, safe place to grow and blossom. Creating that space is, I believe with all my heart, both the joy and the most sacred duty of a marriage.

Photo by Kimberly Stephens

Jean Brashear is an award-winning, bestselling author of nearly thirty romance novels. Her bestselling breakout women's fiction novel is *The Goddess of Fried Okra,* described by one reviewer as "Eudora Welty meets Sue Monk Kidd and they lunch with Fannie Flagg." Please visit her website at www.jeanbrashear.com.

Meryl Sawyer

It's Not What You Say but How You Say It

I was in my midtwenties when I met Jeff, and I'd had other serious boyfriends. Too often, I had to be the one to plan *Everything*. They would do it and pay for whatever but seldom came up with ideas that didn't have to do with sports, like going to a football game.

What works well in a dating situation doesn't always translate the same way in a marriage. The first year we were married, I thought Jeff was way too "bossy" because he wanted to help plan everything from meals to mowing the lawn to weekend social activities. He always wanted to do everything. You could also say he was a micromanager. I thought this was great when we were dating.

Because he had a perfectionist streak, I found that he often "helped" me do whatever I'd agreed to do. For example, we couldn't afford a gardener so we took turns mowing our small yard. Jeff would come out and tell me—while I was sweating and mowing—that it would be better to go in vertical lines rather than horizontal.

If I planned a football party and bought hot dogs to grill at half time, he would pop up at the last minute and say we should have hamburgers. Now, he wasn't expecting me to run off to the supermarket. He would do it but you can see how irritating this would be and how it would change everything.

Somewhere toward the end of the first year, I sat him down and explained how I felt. Looking back, I realize my mother's advice on this was what made it work. DON'T ACCUSE. Don't say you upset me no end when you insist on planning everything and doing it your way. Say: I appreciate how helpful you are. In other words, accentuate the positive. You have great ideas and boundless energy.

But sometimes I would like to sit back at the end of the day and know you had the opportunity to relax while I planned and did everything. I then suggested that we plan by the month, which we were already doing as I was working and so was he, and divide up the activities. He would plan some and if he needed assistance I would do it his way. I would plan other events and if I needed help, I would do it his way.

This worked perfectly. Okay, I had to remind him in the beginning that this was my event or task and to "chill," as we would say today, while I did it. Eventually, it evolved into a division of labor. I did all the social planning and most of the parties in our home. I was *always* careful to ask his input and see what he wanted to do.

As my late mother would say, it's not what you say but how you say it.

The easiest thing to accept about Jeff was that he watched money carefully and never went into debt. I had been raised as an only child of a single parent where money was always tight. My mother handled everything. I had one year on my own before marriage and I must admit that I was working and didn't budget. I didn't overspend but I was conscious of this. When we married we talked about finances even before the wedding. And we set goals. We knew we needed to save to buy a home and that meant mowing the lawn at our rental and not taking exotic vacations. We worked out a budget to see where money was going and how we could cut expenses. I never clipped a coupon but I learned. We bought a house right on schedule and went on to enjoy our lives.

I didn't know it then, but later I read that money is the chief reason couples argue or it's one of the top anyway. Well, we never had an argument because we discussed it early on and dealt with it immediately. Once, and only once, we had to do a partial payment on our credit card. We pinched pennies like crazy the next month so we could pay it off and never had to make a partial payment again.

I would say from my personal experience, that learning to talk to your partner in a loving nonaccusatory way is essential to making your marriage last.

Meryl Sawyer is the *New York Times* and *USA Today* bestselling author of more than twenty romantic suspense novels, one historical novel, and one anthology. Meryl has won the Romantic Times Career Achievement Award for Contemporary Romantic Suspense as well as the award for Best New Contemporary author. She was twice a finalist in the Romance Writers of America's RITA Award. Meryl lives in Newport Beach, California, with her golden retriever. Please visit her website at www.merylsawyer.com.

Shirl Henke

First Dates Can Last a Lifetime

As an impressionable nineteen-year-old college sophomore I was invited by a twenty-three-year-old classmate to attend "a conservative orgy." It was an orgy all right, but it was not conservative! Jim was an "older man" who had spent four years in the Navy. Since he worked full-time, yet made the dean's list, I knew he was intelligent, and all the girls agreed he was good looking in a dark, dangerous way. How could a future romance writer resist?

The evening began tamely enough as I met a group of his friends at a political fund-raiser. They had brought coolers filled with champagne. Several guys who popped corks shot them across the gym like stinger missiles. Jim opened a bottle but aimed his upward. The cork hit a beam fifteen feet overhead and came flying back. Without moving from his seat, he raised his hand and the cork flew directly into it. He turned to the gaping assembly and said nonchalantly, "That's how it's done." I swear I am not making this up.

I was blown away by his sophistication, but starving by the time the party ended as no one had brought food. When they all agreed to meet at a place called Friendly's, I thought food at last! Nope, it was a bar. At one AM the kitchen had closed . . . not friendly! Since no burger or pizza was in sight, I ordered a Coke, then went upstairs to the powder room with the very pregnant wife of one of Jim's friends. Just as we reached the top step a brawl erupted at the bar below. Jackie's husband was in the thick of it. Swinging her huge handbag over her head, she charged down the stairs, shrieking, "Don't you hurt my husband!"

I stood frozen, watching the melee below until Jim came dashing up the steps and said, "The bartender says I've got to get the 'kid' out of here before the cops arrive. Let's go!"

We reached his car just as the sound of sirens echoed down the street. By the time Jim drove me home, dawn was breaking. My mother waited at the front door with murder in her eyes. She had been wary of him because he was an ex-sailor and far too worldly for her innocent daughter. I was grounded for a month, but Jim kept running into me after classes "by accident," asking if I would go out with him again.

At that point, I sort of agreed with my mother. He was wild and much too handsome for my own good. But he was a charming devil and I finally said yes. This time he arrived to pick me up bearing flowers, wearing a gorgeous tailored suit. He took me to a fancy restaurant for a steak dinner. Then we attended a Shakespearean play, which he knowledgeably critiqued. Now I was really off balance. Later, we talked about politics and literature, even favorite foods. I found out he had been cooking since he was in grade school and learned to iron his own clothes in the Navy. Some wild man!

After four years we finally got married. But he put our marriage to quite a few tests, beginning with the move to Seattle to pursue his Ph.D. I am, as my best friend says, "a lizard on a hot rock," a lover of warm summers and short winters, born and raised in St. Louis. Seattle was paradise—for the first month. Then the rain started and the beautiful mountains and bay vanished under a blanket of dense fog! After becoming a "Ph-Deity" Jim accepted a job in the Northeast where deep snow blanketed the ground for eight months of the year! I could've killed him.

After twenty-seven years in exile, I got to return home when he accepted an early retirement. We bought and furnished the home of my dreams, surrounded by woods but only a half-hour from the Gateway Arch. After four years in the Air Force our son Matt moved here and now lives nearby. During a recent family gathering, somebody recounted one of Jim's wilder adventures. Matt, who had heard many stories, asked, "Dad, was that true?" After a minute, Jim said, "Yeah, it happened."

Matt shook his head. "Sorry, Dad, Mom's right. You'd have been dead in a gutter if she hadn't married you."

Well at least one Henke male understands the redemptive powers of love . . . even if the other is still a blockhead.

Shirl Henke has the dubious distinction of working for more publishers than are in existence today. Under her own name she has written more than thirty romance novels, and two thrillers as Alexa Hunt. Twice a RITA finalist, she has won seven RT Awards and appeared on numerous bestseller lists. Please visit her website at www.shirlhenke.com.

Lorraine Heath

The Realist and the Dreamer

When Nathan and I got married more than thirty years ago, we had approximately thirty-five dollars in our checking account. In hindsight, we realize that getting married when we were both slinging pizza with no prospects for better employment opportunities was incredibly stupid. I'd acquired my bachelor's degree in psychology from the University of Texas where we met. He still had many hours to go before he'd earn his bachelor's in accounting.

But ah, young love.

Several months later, I began working as a tax examiner for the IRS. It put me on the path of working for the federal government for twenty-four years. Two years later, Nathan took a position with Texas Instruments and he'd eventually retire from the company.

But we had many roads to travel before that retirement.

For as long as I could remember, I'd yearned to write a novel. I'd even shared with Nathan a time or two my dream of being a writer, to which he'd blithely reply, "You'll never get published."

Still, he didn't complain when I bought an expensive electric typewriter with a correcting ribbon. I used it for pretty much everything except writing the novel of my heart.

Almost fifteen years later, while preparing to travel to Chicago for the government, I popped into a bookstore to purchase something to read on the plane. I wasn't much of a reader, never found anything that truly grabbed me, and I certainly had no desire to read a romance. I knew what happened in those books. I was browsing the *New York Times* bestseller section when I ran across a book with flowers on the cover that piqued my interest. It was *Morning Glory* by LaVyrle Spencer.

I was halfway finished with the story that captivated me when I began to wonder if it was a romance. It was most definitely a love story, but was it a romance? By the time I returned from my trip, I'd read *Morning Glory* three times. When I went to the bookstore to purchase more books by LaVyrle Spencer, my worst literary fears were realized. I had indeed read a romance. But I loved it. Within a month, I'd read everything LaVyrle had written, but more important I finally knew the type of story I wanted to write—I wanted to write stories that would touch the heart.

On my typewriter, with its correctable ribbon, I began writing *Patron of the Hearts*. When it was finished, it comprised only eighty pages and needed a lot of work, but it had a beginning, a middle, and an end, and I knew that I could write a story.

But it was no fun to revise on a typewriter and to retype everything so I started working on another story. Then another. And another. Drafts all, nothing final.

Then one day, I came home from work and discovered a computer in place of my typewriter. Nathan had decided I was serious about writing, and while it put a strain on our budget, he bought me the computer. He still didn't think I'd ever get published, but maybe I could revise and finish a story with a computer rather than a typewriter.

I immediately sat down and began writing a story that I called *Tender Embrace*. When it was finished, revised, and polished, I sent it off to a publisher. Many months later, I received a rejection notice. I decided I needed an agent. A month later I received a very nice rejection from the agent to whom I'd submitted. When I shared the encouraging rejection letter—he liked my writing, just didn't think he could find a market for the story—Nathan said, "I don't think you'll ever get published, but writing is good therapy for you."

Until that moment, I hadn't realized I needed therapy.

I decided one of us needed a little attitude adjustment. He'd never read anything I'd written. How could he know I'd never get published?

He looked at me and said, "I'm sure you're a terrific writer. But the odds are against you."

I scoffed. "Oh, if that's it, no problem. I don't believe in statistics."

In the fall of 1993, I acquired an agent. February 27, 1994, I sold *Tender Embrace*, which was retitled *Sweet Lullaby*, debuted to glowing reviews, and was a finalist for the RITA, Romance Writers of America's most prestigious award. When I returned from the RWA conference in 1997 with a RITA for my fourth book, *Always to Remember,* Nathan greeted me at the airport and said, "I will never doubt your dreams again."

For me, romance isn't flowers and candlelit dinners and whispered sweet nothings. It's small moments that blend together to create a portrait of love. Love is seeing someone reach for a dream you're not sure she'll ever be able to touch, not wanting to see her hurt, but letting her reach. Nathan sought to keep me grounded so my disappointments wouldn't be so great, yet all the while he provided me with the means to keep reaching.

He's always been my most ardent supporter—doing the laundry, the grocery shopping, the cooking—so I could concentrate on my writing, my dream.

Several years ago, he told me not to dedicate a book to him until one of my books landed on the *New York Times*. In 2006, I dedicated *A Duke of Her Own* "To my realist, from your dreamer, with love always."

When *USA Today* and *New York Times* bestselling author **Lorraine Heath** received her bachelors of arts degree in psychology from the University of Texas, she had no idea she had gained a foundation that would help her to create believable characters— characters that are often described as "real people." Her novels have received numerous awards, including the RITA, Romance Writers of America's most prestigious award for excellence. For more info about her or her books, visit www.lorraineheath.com.

Heather Graham

Falling in Love Is Easy;
Staying in Love Is Hard Work

Desire, chemistry, and exciting, fascinating crushes are easy. Falling in love is easy, after all, we're in love with just the thought of falling in love.

Marriage isn't as easy. The dream is, of course, finding that perfect someone. The someone with whom you want to share a family, vacations, dreams, work, the someone who will listen when the world is being cruel, who will understand and be there through all trials and tragedies, and someone with whom you also long to celebrate every great and wonderful triumph in life.

But we're all different, and, as we know, one man's passion may be another man's poison.

The person you first fell in love with and wanted to share everything with may begin to aggravate you. You love mountains, he's into the sea, you begin to think a European vacation would be the cat's meow and he has no desire to speak another language, not even so far as to say, "Bonjour!"

But that's where everything you hear about compromise comes in. I don't believe that people should be forced to stay together when too many things in the world have ripped them apart. But

I also believe that divorce has become far too easy, that it's something envisioned before the wedding bells have ceased to ring.

They (whoever "they" are!) are not kidding when they say that marriage is compromise. And, of course, this is all easier to see from a distance. I remember at the beginning that I was not my mother-in-law's favorite person—I was in theater, and those theater people, *hm*, well, you know. . . . And there were the little edgy family things. I call them the olive oil–butter wars.

His family is very Italian. My dad was Scottish, and my mother fresh off the boat Irish, from Dublin. My mom, at dinner, would be polite, but comment that she just couldn't eat a salad because there was nothing but olive oil on it. Vice versa. My mother-in-law couldn't eat vegetables with that touch of butter. Odd, in the end, before my mom died, the olive oil–butter thing was still going on—but they were best friends. And I adore my mother-in-law.

When I was younger, nothing good was ever easy. But some traumas can be solved easily. We both adored our parents and were very proud of our backgrounds. My mom bought salad oil for when the Pozzesseres came. And Nana Lena bought a few other salad dressings.

Most things are not this easy, but some huge bones of contention are. Now, on many things, Dennis and I are never going to agree. Maybe we agreed on the most important one. Our kids. We both adore them. We didn't even agree on what to do regarding them half of the time, but we also knew one thing deep down no matter what—we both loved them. But that's important to know from the beginning, and since other lives will come to matter, it's not just a matter of agreeing or disagreeing. It's tragic to see the way that children become pawns in marital games. Talking about children before a marriage might be one of the most important things to do—ever.

Is my life, my romance, perfect? Never. I like to say that Dennis has given me lots of conflict to write about! He likes to tease me when I get too busy, reminding me that I can't write on memory forever.

Do we get along now? Nope. He likes mountains. I love the sea. And it is such with many things. I don't believe that I'm really all that scatterbrained—I'm just dealing with the million and one things on my plate all the time and as a friend says, I just don't have enough RAM to get it all processed all of the time.

Dennis has learned to work around me, and make sure he has my total attention when something is really important. He is stubborn. He can drive me crazy. Well, "they" also talk about Italian stubbornness and Irish tempers. But in our house, we can have passionate arguments about who was or wasn't in a movie. Or about the temperature on a certain day, or any other silly thing.

We all know we need to stop. We don't always. But we know, too, that the love is there, and that, if you fight with a family member, it's okay. They do love you, they will forgive you.

Sometimes, I tease that we're just too tired and worn out to do anything else but stay together. But no one is that tired or worn out. We've weathered tragedy, we've had tremendous happiness. We are totally separate, and even hide a bit when we're doing something that's going to drive the other crazy. Sometimes, we'll purposely not ask. But I think that despite all the difficulties, working through them in whatever way helps keep the dream in sight.

My husband and I have not traveled the path that we intended; we probably missed a few important forks in the road. But I am going to grow old with him. When the mind slips and the flesh fades, when beauty is memory, when passion is warmth, the love remains. We are who we are, and we are different, and all this brings me back to what "they" say.

Compromise. And never, never forget that there was love, and when you search beneath the rubble of discontent and anger, it is most often still there. Falling in love is easy; staying in love is hard work. All good things are!

Photo by Charles Bush

Heather Graham is the *New York Times* and *USA Today* bestselling author of more than a hundred novels including suspense, paranormal, historical, and mainstream Christmas fare. She lives in Miami, Florida. Travel, research, and ballroom dancing keep her sane; she is the mother of five, and also resides with two dogs, a cat, and an albino skunk. She is CEO of Slush Pile Productions, a recording company and production house for various charity events. Look her up at www.heathergraham.tv, www.originalheathergraham.com, or www.eheathergraham.com.

Shana Galen

Sports Are Stranger Than Fiction

Almost five years ago, I married a man I like to call Ultimate Sports fan (USF). I think the nickname speaks for itself, but recently I asked USF if there are any sports he doesn't like. We were lying in bed and it was dark, so I couldn't see his expression. But I could tell he was thinking hard because of the long silence.

Finally, he said, "I don't like watching planes race."

"Is that even a sport? Plane racing?" I'm sure it has some fancy name, but he's given up trying to correct me—they're called runs in baseball not points!

"They show it on Fox Sports Southwest every few days. I don't watch it." Almost as an afterthought he added, "I don't watch bass fishing either."

But I kind of had the feeling he was wavering about the bass fishing, not quite ready to commit to actively disliking it.

Okay. So no plane racing (which I'm still not convinced is a sport) or bass fishing. If you ask me if there are any sports I don't like my answer will be all of them. I honestly can't think of a single sport I do like, but I haven't seen plane racing, so I'll reserve judgment on that one.

I, of course, am a romance writer. I've probably never seen

plane racing because I prefer to read or write over watching TV. USF doesn't like to read very much. He reads about sports and skims the paper online, but I can't remember the last time he read a fiction novel.

Obviously whoever coined the phrase opposites attract had us in mind. Because we did attract and pretty much instantly.

Before I was Shana Galen and fellow writer Sophie Jordan was Sophie Jordan, she invited me to her birthday party at Fish, a restaurant in Houston. She also invited her husband's best friend from college. I sort of knew it was a set-up, but I went anyway because it wasn't like I was dating anyone or had any prospects. That's the problem with being a romance writer. You don't meet a lot of real people, only characters.

The first time I saw USF, I didn't pay a whole lot of attention, until he implied I should pay for everyone's meal at Fish being that I was going to be a famous, published writer (I had just sold my first book). I was less than charmed.

But when we all traipsed to a nearby bar, Sophie convinced me to try a Long Island Ice Tea, and I was able to forgive USF for his faux pas. We ended up talking for hours. I can't remember the topics as by then I think I'd had two Long Island Ice Teas, but I know at some point I was hoping he'd kiss me. He was tall, and I have a thing for tall men. And he had such beautiful green eyes. And he really seemed to listen to me. He finally did kiss me. I was sitting on his lap—blame it on the ice tea—and he was playing Ms. PacMan. It was the softest, sweetest first kiss I'd ever experienced.

On the way home—Sophie's husband was driving, no worries—I said, "Well, is he going to call me?"

Everyone agreed USF was the kind of guy to call.

I said, "I guess I'd better go buy the wedding dress then."

Nine months later, he proposed and I did buy that wedding dress.

I often write heroes and heroines who are polar opposites. She's impulsive; he's a thinker. He's a dandy of the first order; she could care less if she dresses in sackcloth. I sometimes wonder what my characters' lives are like after I write The End.

I don't have to wonder very much because I know what it's like to live with your opposite.

It's frustrating and funny and loud and challenging.

You constantly search for common ground, and when you find it, it's always new territory. You constantly explain yourself and yet have the security of knowing this person understands you better than anyone else.

And you're never bored. There's always something new to learn, something you hadn't expected and maybe hadn't even known about.

Plane racing, anyone?

Shana Galen is the author of fast-paced adventurous Regency historical romances, including the RITA-nominated *Blackthorne's Bride*. Her books have been sold worldwide, including Brazil, Russia, Spain, Turkey, and the Netherlands, and have been featured in the Rhapsody and Doubleday Book Clubs. A former English teacher in Houston's inner city, Shana now writes full time. She's a wife, a mother, and an expert multitasker. She loves to hear from readers. Visit her website at www.shanagalen.com.

Stella Cameron
Loving Is the Answer

When I'm told by someone in a relationship that they never argue, I wince. How can two people agree on every point? They can't. That comment probably means that (in my humble opinion) these are two people who suffer in silence, perhaps with smiles on their faces, but who convince themselves that a couple shouldn't disagree, especially in front of anyone else.

Where, I wonder, do I come up with these conclusions? I've been there. In the early years of our marriage, Jerry did voice his feelings, while I remained silent except to tell him that he was right and I needed to shape up.

Short pause here while I scream at the recollection.

I had to change, not to become confrontational, but to boost my sense of self. My announcement that I had signed up for assertiveness training at a local college may have shocked Jerry more than almost anything else in our long marriage.

Over fairly bitter objections, I took that class and followed it up with a class on learning how to play. Sounds nuts? When you play with adults the way you play with children, there is a huge barrier to overcome. As adults, we aren't comfortable letting go, laughing, and being silly. We certainly might not choose to play

READER/CUSTOMER CARE SURVEY

We care about your opinions! Please take a moment to fill out our online Reader Survey at **http://survey.hcibooks.com**. As a **"THANK YOU"** you will receive a **VALUABLE INSTANT COUPON** towards future book purchases as well as a **SPECIAL GIFT** available only online! Or, you may mail this card back to us.

(PLEASE PRINT IN ALL CAPS)

First Name _____ MI. _____ Last Name _____

Address _____ City _____

State _____ Zip _____ Email _____

1. Gender
- ☐ Female ☐ Male

2. Age
- ☐ 8 or younger
- ☐ 9-12 ☐ 13-16
- ☐ 17-20 ☐ 21-30
- ☐ 31+

3. Did you receive this book as a gift?
- ☐ Yes ☐ No

4. Annual Household Income
- ☐ under $25,000
- ☐ $25,000 - $34,999
- ☐ $35,000 - $49,999
- ☐ $50,000 - $74,999
- ☐ over $75,000

5. What are the ages of the children living in your house?
- ☐ 0 - 14 ☐ 15+

6. Marital Status
- ☐ Single
- ☐ Married
- ☐ Divorced
- ☐ Widowed

7. How did you find out about the book?
(please choose one)
- ☐ Recommendation
- ☐ Store Display
- ☐ Online
- ☐ Catalog/Mailing
- ☐ Interview/Review

8. Where do you usually buy books?
(please choose one)
- ☐ Bookstore
- ☐ Online
- ☐ Book Club/Mail Order
- ☐ Price Club (Sam's Club, Costco's, etc.)
- ☐ Retail Store (Target, Wal-Mart, etc.)

9. What subject do you enjoy reading about the most?
(please choose one)
- ☐ Parenting/Family
- ☐ Relationships
- ☐ Recovery/Addictions
- ☐ Health/Nutrition
- ☐ Christianity
- ☐ Spirituality/Inspiration
- ☐ Business Self-help
- ☐ Women's Issues
- ☐ Sports

10. What attracts you most to a book?
(please choose one)
- ☐ Title
- ☐ Cover Design
- ☐ Author
- ☐ Content

HEFG

TAPE IN MIDDLE; DO NOT STAPLE

NO POSTAGE NECESSARY IF MAILED IN THE UNITED STATES

BUSINESS REPLY MAIL
FIRST-CLASS MAIL PERMIT NO 45 DEERFIELD BEACH, FL

POSTAGE WILL BE PAID BY ADDRESSEE

Health Communications, Inc.
3201 SW 15th Street
Deerfield Beach FL 33442-9875

FOLD HERE

Comments

"roll over" where the whole class stretches out on the floor, all sides touching the strangers beside you, before the person on one end rolls over the entire line of bodies, over and over! I feared I might die of embarrassment, instead I laughed until I cried.

Learning to be confident, but not aggressive was a gift to our marriage. In time we came closer and closer together and a mutual respect for opinions and needs grew. I think equality in a relationship is essential. If it isn't there, one partner will forever be unhappy.

And so we come to a goodly number of years later, with three children and three grandchildren. The memories fill every corner, every move we make. How often we talk about the things that are special to us, and laugh over some of the mistakes we made along the way.

Jerry and I like to travel. There is never a road trip when we don't remind ourselves of the incredible number of miles we've driven, side-by-side. We recall driving across the country with our firstborn, Matthew, in an old beater of a Rambler. Matt showed signs of getting sick and became more so. In Pendleton, Oregon, he was running a high fever (we parked by the curb outside a drugstore until it opened) and had to look for a doctor. When I came out of the drugstore with a recommendation for a doctor, and something to help with Matt's fever, Jerry was standing by the curb while the contents of our radiator ran down the gutter. . . .

We got through, and now we have something else to shake our heads over.

But what's really important is "now." Living in the past is a bad idea. We keep our recollections but make sure we're having happy times, and making the best of every day.

We are best friends, confidantes, champions, and we love each other like crazy. My heart still flips when Jerry walks through the door and the best part of the day is when we get into bed and feel so close—even if dog, Millie, and cat, Mango, do regard this time as open season trampoline practice, with Jerry and I as the trampolines.

Love is a decision, it's also a necessity for humans to survive and thrive. Love heals sadness. Love makes the outrageous seem possible. Love changes the heart and soul. Love changes everything.

Photo by Kirsten Phillippe

Stella Cameron is the award-winning, *New York Times, USA Today, Washington Post* bestselling author of more than seventy novels and novellas. Stella has won the Romantic Times Career Achievement Award for Romantic Suspense and the Romantic Times best Romantic Suspense of the Year Award. She has been a RITA finalist and is the recipient of the Pacific Northwest Writers' Association Achievement Award for distinguished professional achievement and for enhancing the stature of the Northwest literary community. Please visit her website at www.stellacameron.com.

Linda Wisdom

Falling in Love

How many movies show that scene where the hero or heroine looks across the room and knows that the person standing there is meant just for them?

And we sit there and sigh along with that secret smile that hints we know just how those characters feel.

My husband likes to say his first sight of me was a red-haired flash racing through the Sears Catalog Store stockroom to the time clock. I always did tend to cut it close. We were married almost two years later.

We worked together for a little over a year before he asked me out on a date. Did it go well? *Hmmm*, not exactly, because the dummy forgot that his ex-girlfriend still expected to go with him to the frat party and he didn't feel he could tell her no.

Obviously, I gave him a second chance, though at the time I wasn't thinking that way.

But it was easy to get even with him, since I was his boss on nights I was in charge of the small catalog store. And we did manage our first date. A drive-in movie where I also brought my puppy. After all, shouldn't every girl have her own private guard dog even if he only weighed a few pounds?

But I think what really made our romance special was that,

after my husband joined the Coast Guard, he later sent me a letter in Morse code. He asked me to marry him. I liked to joke that putting the proposal in writing made it binding. Unfortunately, due to our moves that letter is now gone. It's a shame because it was something very special.

We've been married for thirty-eight years and definitely had a lot of ups and downs over that time. But it's also made us stronger. Especially once I started writing full-time in 1980.

Writers will tell you that their lives can be like a roller coaster. We're guided by the stories running through our imaginations, the feverish writing, sometimes at all hours of the day and night, deadlines, and promotion once the books are released.

It's a lot of give and take, but that's what marriage is all about, isn't it? It's also a learning process, especially when you're opposites.

He's a morning person. No one in the world dare talk to me until I've had enough coffee to be coherent and if I had my way I'd probably sleep until noon. He's very logical. I'm not. Creative personality, remember? He'd rather sleep in a cave with the blinds tightly closed. I love having them open.

Yes, it means compromise, but that's what it's all about. And not about giving up something either, because there are many times that middle ground works even better. Keeping any relationship full and rich is a lot of work, but it's worth it.

Someone once asked my husband how it was being married to a writer. He told them it was never boring.

That's how I feel, too. Our life together is never boring.

Photo by Florian Kucheran

Award-winning **Linda Wisdom** sold her first two novels in 1979. She is presently writing a paranormal series and her books have been optioned for film and television. She lives with her husband and their furry and feathery brood in Murrieta, California. She can be found at www.lindawisdom.com.

Jill Marie Landis

Exceptional Moments of Love

The one thing I truly appreciate about my husband is that his love is constant. After thirty-nine years of marriage filled with all the usual ups and downs, we're still together. He continues to look at me as if I hung the moon. Oh, not all the time, of course, but usually when I'm dancing hula or we are out together. He only has eyes for me—and vice versa.

I love him because he's a child at heart and so am I. When I'm tired or in a bitchy mood, he'll come in and say, "Get up. Come outside. Now." If I balk he insists. "You have to." I whine and grumble or nag—whichever suits the mood—and he keeps it up until he gets me outside and hands me the baseball glove he bought me for Christmas a few years back. Then he runs a few yards away, turns, and starts tossing a softball to me.

Who can stay cranky outside in the sunshine tossing a softball back and forth? Not me, that's for sure, and he knows it. The simple, childhood activity makes me feel like a kid again and always lifts my mood.

Tossing a softball together might not sound very romantic, but every time I use the glove, I recall the day we were attending my niece's softball game and he heard me say, "I've never had a baseball glove of my own. I used to always have to borrow one."

Months later, to my surprise, he actually remembered and surprised me with my own glove at Christmas. I cried when I opened the box and saw that pristine glove. Most of the time I think he's not listening, which is true for most married couples, I think. The fact that he was listening is what makes those moments in the yard and that gift so special.

He's definitely a jock and not exactly a candlelight and flowers kind of guy. But he's a man who remembers his wife never had a baseball glove of her own and then gets one for her. That's a romantic in my book.

Being so into sports and physical activities is his thing and not mine. I'm a sitter (one has to be to type all day). But we've found a way to meld our differences. If there's a piece of sporting good equipment that he can buy, he has it. He surfs, kite boards, paddles an outrigger canoe, lifts weights, swims, skis, and plays golf. I watch and cheer him on—except for the golf—which I consider long precious hours for me to write without interruption. Unlike some wives, I *love* golf.

He has a habit of constantly talking about upgrading this or that piece of sporting goods equipment. He "desperately" needs a new outrigger canoe, or whatever. A few years ago, I noticed we were never upgrading anything in the house, like the sofa or refrigerator. We never upgraded things like that without my taking action. Then I started using his own terminology. I tried the phrase, "Honey, we need to upgrade the stove." He finally understood and married life got a little easier. Sometimes all it takes is communicating in the same language.

Because he's in shape, he wears the same size clothes he wore when we got married. I won't go there regarding the things in my closet. Since he does some modeling and acting, his physical shape is important to his work. He doesn't even have to try and he never gains a pound. He works out because he actually wants to. What's this all got to do with romance? I know he loves me because he's married to a woman who is half Italian and doesn't like to sweat unless I'm lying out in the sun on a beach towel.

He's such a head over heels romantic and so in love with me that he's loved me through thin and thick. The feeling is mutual.

Photo by Sara Wall

Jill Marie Landis's twenty-five novels have earned distinguished awards and slots on the *USA Today* Top 50 and the *New York Times* Bestsellers Plus. She is a seven-time Romance Writers of America RITA Award Finalist in both Single Title Historical and Contemporary Romance, as well as a Golden Heart and RITA Winner. Jill Marie resides in Hawaii with her husband. When she's not writing or sitting on the beach reading, she enjoys family and friends, raising orchids, plunking on the ukulele, dancing the hula, and quilting. Visit her at www.jillmarielandis.com.

Elizabeth Boyle

When Opposites Attract

I've always sort of envied couples who are joined at the hip. You know the ones I mean, you see them shopping together, off having coffee, sharing confidences, they do everything together. You can't think of one without the other. They live to be together.

As the ads for computer dating tell us, we should all have this perfect mate, this match that fits us, the one person who loves everything we do and is compatible in every way. And I am here to proudly declare and defend that old adage: Opposites Attract.

My husband and I are nearly complete opposites. Literally. He's conservative, I'm quite liberal. I was raised in a hippy loving family in the Pacific Northwest and he is the product of a solid Midwest upbringing. I love the arts and the subtleties of foreign films; he is an engineer and loves hard facts and Forensic Files. He sees a garden and admires the cut of the lawn, I go into joy over the flowers in the beds beyond.

And yet, from the moment we met, we've shared a unique attraction and respect for the other that held us together as we dated for years, which led to much head shaking as we decided to get married, and even more wonder as we recently celebrated our seventeenth wedding anniversary. To all the naysayers who never thought we would last because of our different natures, I say "Ha!"

For us, being opposites is what works best and I think that is because what we do share are strong independent streaks. We each blaze our own trails in our own professions, have our interests, and don't mind doing things on our own. And sometimes, we prefer to do them just that way: alone. That desire to be separated has never led to hurt feelings or misunderstandings, since we both value our own individual time and respect each other's need for it.

I think that word, *respect,* is what has always been at the core of our relationship. A deep and abiding respect for our individual strengths (I cook, he cleans; I nurture and coordinate, he fixes and repairs; he rarely gets lost, I can parallel park) brings balance to our lives. And it isn't only respect, but an understanding and a valuing of the other's capabilities and a fair acknowledgment of our own weaknesses. With each other, those weaknesses are not failures as we have one another to pick up where the other falters.

Nowhere did that become clearer than when we had our children, and mostly because of our second child, Matthew, who has autism. This profound diagnosis, this child that God gave us, has shown us quite clearly why we work as a couple. There are days when the demands of raising a special needs child are completely overwhelming, when the tantrums, the bills, the far-flung therapy appointments, the constant challenges are just too much, and on those days, when one of us succumbs to tears, to agony, to just plain despair, the other one is there to step in. Faithfully, purposefully, and with the strength of commitment that the other has lost, at least for the short term. If we were joined at the hip, this would never work.

Oh, don't get me wrong, we have our battles, our deep divisions. Being polar opposites can mean some very strong and loud differences (and since we are both Irish, that means really loud). But we always find our way back to the middle because we know that whatever the other's opinion, we have each other's best interests at heart.

Sometimes I like to think of our marriage as exactly like the symbol of yin and yang, the light and the dark. Because when you put those opposites together, they fit perfectly into a whole, which is how you should feel in a marriage. A funny thing that fitting together—for years I was always cold at night and would seek him out in the bed to cuddle up to for warmth. And now, as I've reached a certain age, I am always hot. But like true opposites, my husband now finds himself cold at night, and once again, our differences make us whole as he whispers to me, "I'm freezing," and I can happily offer him all the warmth he needs.

Elizabeth Boyle is the *New York Times* bestselling author of eighteen historical romance novels. In addition to her love affair with happy endings and all things Jane Austen, she loves to cook, knit, and garden—when not chasing after her boys. Visit Elizabeth at www.elizabethboyle.com.

Geri Buckley Borcz
What About Opposites?

My husband and I are proof that opposites attract. We're both strong personalities, but we complement each other because we're opposites in strengths and weaknesses.

For instance, Gene loves to cook but hates cleaning, while I don't mind cleaning but hate to cook. He adores inviting family and friends over for a good meal, and early on in our marriage, it was nothing for me to get home from work and discover upwards of a dozen people staying for dinner. But I'll admit that kind of hospitality took some getting used to.

You see, Gene's from a family of Polish immigrants who welcome visitors with hugs and kisses and an offer of plenty to eat and drink. My family, however, weren't especially affectionate or demonstrative people, or even particularly hospitable. I had to step out of my comfort zone and really be open to change, especially since we lived in Gene's hometown.

One of the toughest differences we've coped with in our marriage is that Gene is a workaholic and I'm not. In the beginning, I worked regular hours, while Gene worked different shifts, so when our children came along, the job naturally fell to me to maintain a steady schedule and home routine.

This went on for almost ten years as Gene attended college in his off hours, eventually earning his master's and most of his doctorate degree. Probably the only thing that kept me rooted during this hectic decade was the reminder that our time would be freed up once we had reached certain personal and financial goals. Little did I know it would take sixteen years to bring those goals to fruition.

By that time, Gene was working sixty-to-seventy hours a week and showed no signs of slowing down. We talked about spending more time playing and less time working, and we would do it, but after . . . after the oldest graduated college . . . then after the youngest graduated college . . . then after the kids settled down . . . then after the grandchildren were born. . . .

You get the picture. Gene retired a year ago, and getting him to slow down is still very much a work-in-progress for both of us.

So, if I had to sum up a healthy relationship in one phrase, I would say attitudes and behaviors. Nothing changes until those two things change.

There's a saying that a man falls in love with a woman because of the way he feels about himself when he's with her, and that if we decide not to have a love affair with our man, someone else will. Well, the same holds true for a woman.

Along the way, Gene and I agreed not to settle, not for a mediocre love life, not for a routine relationship, and not for monotony. We're partners not crutches. We've made a commitment to have a love affair for the rest of our lives, and our attitude and behavior reflect that commitment.

Sure, we've faced the same issues all couples have—family, financial, health, employment, and others—but we don't allow what happens to us to determine the quality of our life. It's what we do about what happens that determines the quality of our lives together.

And I'd say what we're doing is working. This year, Gene and I are celebrating forty years together.

Eppie-award winner **Geri Buckley Borcz** writes general fiction short stories, historical and contemporary romance novels, and women's fiction. She lives in Northwest Florida with her husband and their two dogs. Geri's current contemporary romance is *Hot Ticket,* an anthology from Berkley. Please visit her website at www.geribuckley.com.

Mary Balogh
In the Nick of Time

After graduating from university in Wales, my home country, I decided to teach and travel the world at the same time. It was a great time to do that—there was a huge shortage of teachers all over the world. My first stop was Kipling, Saskatchewan, Canada, on a two-year contract.

Kipling, population 1000 at the time, is a small farming town in the middle of the prairies, very different from the British city life I was accustomed to. And teaching high school English was far more demanding than I had anticipated. I found myself trapped in the town by lack of transport and not really having time to go anywhere anyway. I was working long days and half the nights preparing classes and marking tests and essays. I was so unhappy after six months or so that I submitted my resignation, effective the end of June, and was prepared to break my contract for the second year. I was going home!

I bought my airline ticket, but I had a problem. I had come to Canada by ship the previous year, bringing a large trunk with me (yes, all this *was* that long ago). I packed the trunk and tried to send it from the railway station in Kipling, but no one there knew what to do with it. The surcharge on the plane was going to be astronomical. And so it happened that at the end of May both I and all my belongings were still in town when the fateful phone call came.

Robert Balogh had apparently been trying to meet me all year. I was the new teacher in town. I spoke with a strange accent (Welsh), and I wore mini-skirts at a time when prairie schools were starting to ban them among their girl students as well as long hair among the boys. So I suppose I had caused something of a stir. Robert had expected to see me at some town dances or at the local ice arena, where he played goalie with the men's hockey team. But I never appeared—I was always at home trying to make some impression upon that mighty pile of papers waiting to be marked! Finally, in May, he took matters into his own hands and phoned me to invite me to a high school graduation dance in a neighboring town. I had never met him and I'm not sure I had ever gone on a blind date before, but I was a bit fed up after living through a year of almost zero social life. I said yes.

When I asked my landlady if she knew Robert Balogh, she looked blank for a moment and then her face lit up. Yes, yes, he was from a very nice family, and—she stopped to gasp and grasp my arm, "Oh, Mary, he is tall and handsome."

I got ready on the appointed evening, and when my landlady called to say my date had come, I went downstairs to meet him. He was standing in the middle of the kitchen, dressed smartly (people did in those days!) in black slacks, crisp shirt and tie, and dark green blazer. And, yes, he was tall and slim and handsome—and he had the smiling blue eyes that many of the heroes of my books have since inherited.

Is it possible to fall in love at first sight? Well, I believe it is because I did. It takes far longer really to love, of course, and to commit to a long-term relationship, but that gloriously euphoric sensation of tumbling instantly into love is very real.

It has to be, doesn't it? Within a month of that date I had completely changed my life plans. My job had already been taken, of course, but by chance there was a last minute opening to teach social studies in the middle school—and I took it. I used my air ticket to go home to Wales for the summer, but I came back, to be met at the airport by a rather gorgeous man wearing a cowboy hat and boots with more casual clothes than I had seen before. I discovered that over the summer I had not over-glamorized him in memory.

Less than a year after that we were married.

We are still married forty-one years later.

Somewhere along the line that idea of mine of traveling the world, teaching as I went, was sacrificed for something that has proved far more satisfying.

Welsh-born **Mary Balogh** now lives in Saskatchewan, Canada. She has written close to 100 novels and novellas, most of which are set in Regency England and all of which are love stories. They include the *New York Times* bestselling *Slightly, Simply,* and Huxtable series. Please visit her website at www.marybalogh.com.

Kat Martin
For Better or Worse

I think the most important secret to making a relationship last is forgiveness. We all make mistakes. Your spouse is bound to make them and so are you. Don't stay mad. Get the anger out in the open, have your say, and get over it.

Another thing is to accept your partner's faults. This may take some doing. In my case, I am a neat-nik and my husband is a pack rat. We have argued over this endlessly. Fortunately, it is not a deal breaker—or a marriage breaker. Learn to compromise. In this case, I let my husband have his own space, a place where he can be as messy as he wishes. In return, he does his best to keep the rest of the house picked up.

Another good idea is to focus on the good things, the things you love about your spouse. I love my husband's intelligence. I love his creativity, and I love that he is always coming up with new things he wants to do. Since I usually get to go with him wherever these new things lead, it keeps our life interesting. I don't like it when his projects cost too much—I like to save money for the future. But again, we've learned to compromise. As my husband points out, "Have you ever seen an armored car following a hearse?"

As far as romance goes, I think when you're getting along well with your spouse, the romance sort of comes naturally. Go out of town; get away from whatever problems you might be facing at home. It's amazing how just that little break is enough to spark the romantic side of your relationship.

My husband and I have been married twenty-five years. We are still in love. But marriage is work. Keeping that in mind is another secret of a lasting relationship.

Kat Martin is the *New York Times* bestselling author of fifty historical and contemporary romance novels. To date, more than 12 million copies of her books are in print and she has been published in seventeen foreign countries. Kat and her husband, author Larry Jay Martin, spend most of the year on their ranch near Missoula, Montana. Winters are spent at their beach house in Southern California. Kat is currently at work on her next romance novel. Please visit her website at www.katmartin.com.

Jasmine Cresswell
A Romantic Moment

When I was a teenager, back in the days when dinosaurs roamed the earth, I fell passionately in love approximately once a month. I was addicted to the first, tingling kiss and the excitement of a pounding heart and racing pulses. Since I spent only minimal amounts of time actually talking to my boyfriend-of-the-month, his looks were a lot more significant than his personality. Clothes counted, too, I seem to recall. And hair and teeth were especially important.

Even then, when self-awareness was clearly not my strong suit, I noticed that my attraction to a given man always lasted longer if he wasn't obtainable, which suggests that as far as I was concerned, romance had more to do with fantasy than reality. For example, there was a twenty-two-year-old post-grad student from Germany living with one of our neighbors who only had to turn his soulful dark brown eyes in my direction to make my knees tremble and my palms turn sweaty. I was barely seventeen at the time, so of course he was scarcely aware of my existence. Since he rarely spoke to me except to say a cheerful hello, I was free to build whatever fantasies I chose around this unsuspecting young man. To sum it up in a nutshell, romance in those days was all about me; it had nothing to do with a grounded, real-world relationship.

That changed almost instantly when I met Malcolm, my husband-to-be. We're both English by birth, but we met in Rio de Janeiro, Brazil. We first saw each other across a crowded room at a party and there was that amazing instant click of intense physical awareness. Malcolm, always a man to go pretty directly for what he wants, walked up to me and suggested that we should go outside onto the huge balcony that led off the room where the party was being held. "So that we can talk without too many other people around," he said.

Sipping iced drinks, we stood under the starry night sky and looked out over the fabulous views of the city, the coastline, and the surrounding mountains. Surprisingly, despite the underlying hum of attraction between us and the made-to-order romantic surroundings, we did indeed spend the next two hours talking. We exchanged a few biographical facts (how did two Brits end up thousands of miles away in Rio?), but mostly we talked about ideas: religion, politics, the differences between British and Brazilian culture.

Malcolm worked for an international consumer products company and I was working for the British Embassy. Our experiences and worldviews were quite different but we each found the other person strangely fascinating. I was twenty years old at the time (I'd graduated early from high school and college.) Malcolm was twenty-six. Not surprisingly, we had all the arrogance of people who are too young to have had the rough edges knocked off our certainties and we were both quite sure that we knew everything. Apparently, though, we really did know just enough to keep each other interested. We met again the next evening, and the following weekend, and then as often as we could given our hectic work schedules. I think we both knew within a few weeks of our first meeting that we would get married.

Many years of marriage, four children, and twelve grandchildren later, I can honestly say that Malcolm and I still find each other interesting. Of course, we have a lot to talk about aside from politics and religion these days! We're convinced, of course, that our kids are uniquely wonderful and that our grandkids will surpass even our children's amazingly high levels of achievement. The great thing about staying married to the same person is that there's nobody around to drop even a casual hint that we may be delusional.

We still argue passionately about politics, although over the years we've persuaded each other to change views on so many topics that it's amazing we still have anything to discuss. Most of all, we've come to realize that the mere act of living together forges powerful bonds made up of the simple stuff of daily life. Our wealth of shared memories have become a magnet that not only binds our past into a single complex whole, but new events take on a special sheen as they are woven into the fabric of our current lives. Who knew that sitting on the deck of our home in Colorado and watching the sun set as we share a glass of wine before dinner makes for one of life's perfect moments? Perhaps some people would claim that it's also a romantic moment. To me, though, it's not really about romance at all. It changed long ago into something much more important: it changed into love.

Jasmine Cresswell is the *USA Today* and internationally bestselling author of more than sixty novels. Her most recent work has focused on fast-paced, high tension suspense, but her earlier work included a variety of romances, including historicals and three of her personal favorites that have paranormal themes. Jasmine is currently at work on her latest international thriller, *Heiress*. Please visit her website at www.jasminecresswell.com.

Secret Key #5

Second Chances

Death and divorce are grim realities. Yet every day the miracle happens over and over—out of the innumerable known and unknown people in the cosmos, a man and a woman will find each other, love each other. That they can stay together for years at a time, endure the stresses of busy lives, share the pleasures of touch and sensation, and relieve the pains the world inflicts—that surely is a miracle. So many quietly happy marriages and relationships exist around us, men and women who come together in joy and delight, whose spirits are refreshed when they see each other at the end of the day. That's romance! And I have been blessed to live it.

–Nicole Byrd

Barbara Samuel

A View from the Top of the World

The trail is littered with hail the size of quarters and I'm wet and cold as I trudge up the mountain with the person who brought me to help at a water station for one of the most challenging races in the country, the Pikes Peak Ascent. The air is painfully thin. We each have a plastic trash bag, and we're picking up runner-litter. I don't know how anyone runs this trail, but I've just seen hundreds of people do it, and the past two hours were a misery for them. They ran in the hail and lightening, clad only in running shorts and the plastic garbage bags they pulled over their heads. What am I, a middle-aged divorcee who smoked for twenty years, doing up here?

I was married for a long time, nineteen years to the day, and when it fell apart, I was devastated. Afterward, I struggled with ideas of romantic love and what that meant.

But I tend to enjoy the company of other people, and after awhile I found myself out and about again. Sometimes dating, meeting for coffee or a hike, or a meal. I was happy again, finally. I had friends, and loved my work, and traveled around the world. While I liked dating, I was not at all interested in letting anyone close enough to break my heart again.

One late October day, I walked into one of my favorite restaurants and met a man I'd been talking to via e-mail.

When I sat down, I knew it was trouble. He had the kindest, bluest eyes I'd ever seen. What I really wanted to do was flee right out the door, but he ordered a cup of hot chocolate and told me that he loved dogs, so I stayed. He had a posh British accent and wore a beautiful sweater. We agreed to meet again.

And so it went, one more step and one more step. One day, we ate French toast and I told him about my special fascination with blue jay feathers, that they seemed to me to be a signal of answered prayers. Later that same afternoon, we were walking his neighbor's dog around a park, and he bent down to pick something off the grass. "Isn't this a blue jay feather?" he asked, his eyes glittering.

Why yes. Yes it was.

But still, like any smart romantic heroine, I resisted. Not for me the happily ever after, no sirree! He created a place for me to work in peace and quiet in his house. I resisted. He never seemed to mind that I was not particularly slim, that I was a little older, that I had children and five animals. I resisted. He had a goofy laugh and a sense of proportion and calm that balanced my sometimes turbulent artistic personality.

Still, I resisted even admitting to myself that I was madly in love with Christopher Robin.

One of the things that bonded us early on was a love of Pikes Peak, which is the mountain that overlooks Colorado Springs. I loved being on top of the mountain, in the too-thin air, loved being able to look up at the summit from the city and think, Yes, I know what that looks like. He had run the Ascent, one of the hardest races in the country.

As a member of the local running club, he asked me if I'd like to help with the Ascent, too. I was thrilled.

We awakened in the dark of a Saturday morning and met at the base of the mountain and boarded buses that took us to a water station about two miles down, around 12,000 feet. It was a beautiful morning, sunny but sharp so high up, even though it was August. We had on our coats and hats for hours.

It was more fun than I had even imagined. I loved watching the elite runners. I cheered the first women to cross our water station, secretly thrilled to the large numbers of fit middle-aged women (and men) who ran very well. Behind me, I heard Christopher Robin, who was handing out water, call out, "Well done! Well done!" in a hearty voice.

At noon, the clouds rolled in. We eyed them nervously. The most dangerous thing at the top of a mountain is lightening, and this mountain is known for lightening strikes.

But of course, there was nothing to be done. The runners were still coming in a steady stream up the mountain.

We stayed. It began to rain. Then, dreadfully, lightening began to crack down all around us.

Runner after runner came by, wet, cold, faces all masks of misery. The hail banged down on our shoulders and backs, lightening slammed across bare rock faces, so close it raised the hair on my neck and arms.

Finally, the runners were all through. The hail slowed. Christopher Robin poured a cup of tea from his thermos. British tea, hot, strong, and milky, and gave it to me. "This will hold you until we get to the top."

The tendrils of steam hung in the cold air. It warmed me, throat to belly. "Perfect," I said.

"We do a few things very well."

He and I are the last of our group to head back to the top. I'm starving and cold, but at the summit, we find the cafe has not a crumb. The cold, stranded runners have eaten it all.

It's going to be awhile before the buses can take us down, so CR and I wander out to a wall and sit. Clouds hang over head, but they can't obscure the view of the city, thousands of feet below. Tendrils of mist curl around nearby peaks. The mountain itself is blue and pink, burly and astonishing. CR pulls out his thermos and a bagel smeared with butter and Marmite. "Do you want half?"

I will eat anything. He pours the still steaming sweet tea into the cup, and divides the sandwich. Marmite is a salty substance, and I've never liked it, but after the day in the weather, it tastes delicious. The tea is heartening. He looks at me, his eyes as blue as the mountains, and says, "What did you think of your adventure?"

And like any good romance heroine, I finally admit to myself that this is "The One." I think, sometimes it's worth every single minute of drama and struggle and danger to get where you need to be.

Here.

"Well done," I say, and kiss his cold mouth. He puts his arm around me and we admire the view from the top of the world.

Photo by Blue Fox Photography

Barbara Samuel is a multiple RITA award-winning author with more than twenty-five books to her credit, both historical and contemporary romances and women's fiction. Her work has captured a plethora of awards, including four RITAs; the Colorado Center for the Book Award (twice); Favorite Book of the Year from Romance Writers of America, and the Library Journal's list of Best Genre Fiction of the year, among many others. Please visit her website at www.barbarasamuel.com.

Nicole Byrd

Happy Endings

I've always loved happy endings. I want good to defeat evil, as it does in fantasy; order to be restored, as it is in any decent mystery; and, of course, true love to conquer all, as it does in romance.

Does any woman, in her heart of hearts, desire less? Not me!

I want to be cherished, damn it. I want a man who wants an equal, in intelligence, spirit, courage, wit, and most of all, heart. I know that this can, in fact, occur—two people can find each other, can be happy together, can delight each other with equally fiery passions, and face the world's challenges together. This is not expecting too much. In literature, this is not exaggeration or fanciful writing. This is fact. I know, it has happened to me.

I've seen the bad and the good, not just the good, but the best! The first time I married too young and for all the wrong reasons. I'd just had my heart broken and was vulnerable to a good-looking, sexy stranger. He demanded an almost instant commitment. Eloping, we married quick, and almost as soon, I knew I'd made a huge mistake. But by then, the stork was on the way, and I felt I had to try to make it work. That marriage ended inevitably in divorce, and despite the two wonderful children it had engendered, my feelings then would not have permitted me to write a good romance. Gory mysteries, maybe!

I announced to the world that I would never marry again and tried to smother my hurt and loneliness in hard work: teaching and writing on the side and ferrying my children to Scouts and Little League games and dance practice. Despite my protestations, my friends cajoled me into occasional blind dates, usually leaving me only more determined in my resolve. Except there came a date where, in spite of my best intention to be the last single mother standing, I tumbled into love again. Later married again. Moved halfway across the country again.

When you both bring along kids and history and baggage, second marriages have extra challenges, but sometimes you have both learned from earlier mistakes. Sometimes you love enough to work through the inevitable rough spots. Sometimes you are happy, blissfully, quietly. Sometimes the kids do well, and you can settle down as the older ones go off to school and the younger ones develop their own social lives and are no longer constantly underfoot. The two adults can enjoy each other's company, travel now and then. When you're home, make love lavishly in an otherwise empty house!

Life can throw terrible surprises, however: illness that unfairly and abruptly cuts short your happiness, leaving you alone and grieving. So once again, I threw myself into work, this time writing—yes, romance, using the sweet memories to evoke love and laughter for fictional couples who could come together in happy endings, endings that I could ensure would not finish too soon! And glad for my family's good health and success, but always a little wistful, I would go to my children's and stepchildren's college graduations and weddings and new baby appearances, alone.

I realized how blessed I was to have known true love, and my good fortune to have accomplished my lifelong goal, to write and publish books, especially the books I enjoyed—with likable characters, adventurous plots, and, yes, happy endings!

As for myself, I never dreamed that I would experience true love again. At this point in my life, I expected to only enjoy love in the pages of my books—only there to encounter courtly gentlemen and exciting lovers.

In fact, I almost missed the first signs of courtship when a longtime friend, widowed as I was, a writer as I was, discretely signaled that he wanted more than just friendship. When I at last opened my eyes, I was astounded to find that, yes, love can happen at any age. And, as the poet Robert Browning said, sometimes, the best is indeed kept for last. And, what the Victorian poet didn't say, older men can be remarkable lovers!

Death and divorce are grim realities. Yet every day the miracle happens over and over—out of the innumerable known and unknown people in the cosmos, a man and a woman will find each other, love each other. That they can stay together for years at a time, endure the stresses of busy lives, share the pleasures of touch and sensation, and relieve the pains the world inflicts—that surely is a miracle. So many quietly happy marriages and relationships exist around us, men and women who come together in joy and delight, whose spirits are refreshed when they see each other at the end of the day. That's romance! And I have been blessed to live it.

So whether you prefer it in historical costume, in today's world, in the future's hardware, or decked out in myth and legend, romantic love will certainly endure. It touches the deepest chambers of our hearts—stirs the depths of our souls. It reminds us what we care most about. May all of you enjoy true love, too!

Nicole Byrd is a pseudonym for Cheryl Zach and daughter Michele Place. Writing alone, Cheryl is a RWA Hall of Famer and bestselling author for romance and young adults. The highly acclaimed Sinclair Family saga began with *Dear Impostor*—Please visit her website at www.NicoleByrd.com.

Elizabeth Hoyt
The Opposite of Love at First Sight

I met my husband in the summer of 1987 in a hot, sticky, cornfield in Wisconsin and, at first sight, I thought he was a jerk. A humorless, uptight, kind-of-angry jerk.

But I digress.

The reason I was in that cornfield was because I was taking a summer archaeology field course. The reason he was in the cornfield was because he was the teaching assistant (T.A.) for the field school, and the archaeological site we were excavating was the basis for his Ph.D. dissertation. Being in charge of a large, chaotic dig upon which your entire future career rests can make even the most mellow of men cranky. But being a sophisticated twenty year old, I didn't think of that. All I saw was a surly man who had a tendency to bark orders and then stalk abruptly away.

Jerk.

At the end of that summer the field school ended and I might never have thought about that surly T.A. again except that in the spring I took an archaeology curating class. The class involved sitting in a lab for long hours measuring and recording archaeological artifacts. And who should be the T.A. of the class? Why that same surly T.A. from the field school the summer before. Except now he wasn't quite so surly and the longer I talked to him, the nicer he became. When he informed me—very casually—that he wasn't grading me in the course (and thus was free to date me) I took note. When he mentioned in an offhand sort of way (for the third time) that perhaps we should get together some night I replied, "How about Thursday?"

I married my T.A. in the fall of 1988 and although he does occasionally revert to his surly ways, I have been more than happy these last twenty-plus years that I took the time to give him a second look.

Elizabeth Hoyt is a *New York Times* bestselling author of historical romance, including *The Raven Prince*, *To Beguile a Beast*, and *To Desire a Devil*. She also writes deliciously fun contemporary romance under the name Julia Harper. Elizabeth lives in central Illinois with three untrained dogs, two angelic but bickering children, and one long-suffering husband. Please visit her website at www.elizabethhoyt.com.

Ciji Ware

A Marriage of Long Duration

Tony and I married two days after Christmas in 1976. I had been married before and had a son, Jamie, who was nearly four years old.

We plunged into the "fast lane" of L.A. media—in those days I was a news broadcaster on radio and TV and Tony was a financial journalist regularly contributing to several national magazines. We soon found ourselves juggling and struggling to keep our three-ring circus going as freelancers in the same household with different deadlines, lots of obligations to meet, in addition to raising a little boy who had soccer practices, boy scouts, school events, and out-of-town track meets.

This madhouse presented the first "crisis" in our marriage. I had begun to feel I was totally overburdened. When Tony arrived home from an assignment in the Philippines, I remember wailing that I just couldn't keep up this pace. He listened to my litany of complaints and then pointed out, "Well, Ciji, you signed up for all this."

He stopped me dead in my tracks. Yes, of course, it would help if he told his editors he couldn't take every story that sent him to Timbuktoo . . . but then, I didn't have to agree to do five or six jobs at once, never saying *no* to anything.

What probably has saved us at each of the major bumps in the road these thirty-plus years is the fact that we could usually talk things through by revealing to each other how we truly felt. It's taken a long time for us to learn to let the other person finish a sentence and listen carefully to each other in order to figure out what's really at the bottom of any disagreement. Most important, we now allow the other person the dignity of his/her own style and pace in moving through life.

I had to learn that "it's my way or the highway" wasn't the best way to be; to learn I wasn't always right about everything; and to allow Tony to be the loving, caring, thoughtful person he truly is—without my directing everything. I've learned that true romance is appreciating your significant other for exactly who that person is, and not trying to mold him or her into what they (in your view) "should" be.

Tony would probably tell you that true romance also comes from learning it's important to keep commitments, no matter how trivial; to be truly present in relationships that matter; to appreciate and cultivate people who genuinely have our best interests at heart—and to opt out if they do not.

Like most couples in marriages of long duration, we have had our serious ups and downs. However, there is something quite wonderful in still getting a little zing when Tony heads out of the room, dressed in his tuxedo for a party, or arrives home from an adventure with his suitcase in tow and a story to tell.

I am filled with gratitude that we can still laugh so hard, tears stream down our cheeks. Romance, for us, anyway, has endured by not allowing walls of indifference or disdain to divide us.

Intimacy for us has become not only loving each other but also accepting each other. We try to pay attention to the important stuff, release the trivial, strive to share common interests, and revel in the fact that there is always something to talk about that matters to us both.

And that's because we still matter—to each other. Yes, we're grayer . . . not as "gorgeous" as in our sprightly youth, but after all these years of keeping on keeping on, I know who Tony truly is, and he knows me, and our romance has been sustained. Not only because of our shared history, but because we've never lost sight of the essential qualities that drew us together in the first place: mutually-shared curiosity about the world around us and the fun to be had in it, a love of adventure and the "newest new thing," along with a highly-cultivated sense of life's absurdities.

But the real secret? My husband is the only man I was ever attracted to who loves to stop everything at four o'clock and brew us both a cup of tea.

And that, my dears, is sexy!

Photo by Gowdy Thayer

Ciji Ware is a multi-published author of both nonfiction and fiction books, including the historical novels *Island of the Swans, A Cottage by the Sea, Wicked Company,* and her latest work of fiction, *A Race to Splendor*. She is also the best-selling nonfiction author of *Rightsizing Your Life: Simplifying Your Surroundings While Keeping What Matters Most*. Please visit her website at www.cijiware.com.

Secret Key #6

Trust and Respect

People usually associate romance novels first and foremost with passion, but in truth, passion is worthless, even destructive if it's for someone you don't respect or can't trust. Trust and respect can't be given blindly in life or in romance fiction, however, but have to be tested and earned, and then maintained through a track record of proven integrity. Once you are sure of someone's overall integrity, then I think it's wise to have a policy of preemptive forgiveness, so that the little petty annoyances of life don't build up into big things and start to erode away the love. Whenever I start to get aggravated by little things, I just stop for a second and imagine how I'd feel if I lost him. That puts everything into perspective within about two seconds.

–Gaelen Foley

Rachel Gibson
Friends and Lovers

I met my husband, James, on the night we graduated from high school. We both went to the same school but we didn't have mutual friends and had never had a class together. Although I liked him right away because he was very funny and nice, I really wasn't interested in him. I was much too busy running around with my girlfriends to want to settle down in a relationship, but James kept asking me out until I finally said yes.

It was nice. We had a good time and laughed a lot. James has always made me laugh, but I told him I didn't want to go out with him because I didn't want a boyfriend. He said that was fine with him. We'd just be friends. And we were. We were great friends until one day I realized he'd become a huge part of my life. I realized I liked the way he looked in his Levis and Brooks Brothers' dress shirts. I liked the way he made me laugh all the time, and I liked the way he smelled. While he'd been pretending that all he wanted was friendship, he'd been working on making me fall in love with him. And I did.

James and I married when we were both twenty-one. We've been married for twenty-four years, and I think part of the reason we're still married is because we basically grew up together. We are still best friends and he still makes me laugh more than any other person I know. We also take care of each other. If I'm working a lot, he will pack a picnic basket with all my favorite food and drive us somewhere nice. I know that he loves to fish, so I recently bought my first fishing license and pole and I fish with him. I don't really like to fish, but he does. And I like to spend time with him.

I don't think the romantic things that keep a marriage together are the overt and obvious things. It's not the size of the diamond (although a big one is always nice), or the number of roses that matters most. It's the thoughtful little things we do for each other every day that count and keep us together.

Photo by Tana Photography

New York Times bestselling author **Rachel Gibson** writes fast-paced contemporary romances. Four of her novels were named among the Top Ten Favorite Books of the Year by Romance Writers of America. She has won numerous awards, including Borders Bestselling Romantic Comedy, National Reader's Choice, and the RITA award for the Best Single Title Contemporary. When not writing, Rachel can be found boating on Payette Lake, shopping for shoes, or forcing her cat to share her favorite indulgence—Judge Judy. Please visit her website at www.rachelgibson.com.

Gaelen Foley
Show, Don't Tell

My husband is the most important person in my life, and I am grateful to God every day for the gift of my marriage, and for the joy, tenderness, understanding, loyalty, affection, laughter, and stability that Eric has brought into my existence. We met before we were out of our teens, so we really have grown up together. It still mystifies me how both of us knew the very night we met that we had found "the one." From our official first date three days later to this very day, we have been virtually inseparable. (We got married at the same place where we had our first date, by the way—the Phipps Conservatory in Pittsburgh, a huge Victorian glasshouse and botanical gardens. Very romantic!)

Over the past twenty-two years, our relationship has had many ups and downs (and provided lots of fodder for my love stories, ha, ha). To me, the two biggest secrets to a great relationship are trust and respect—as anyone who reads my novels has probably noticed. Both themes are pretty much always there in every book I write. People usually associate romance novels first and foremost with passion, but in truth, passion is worthless, even destructive if it's for someone you don't respect or can't trust.

Trust and respect can't be given blindly in life or in romance fiction, however, but have to be tested and earned, and then maintained through a track record of proven integrity. Once you are sure of someone's overall integrity, then I think it's wise to have a policy of preemptive forgiveness, so that the little petty annoyances of life don't build up into big things and start to erode away the love. Whenever I start to get aggravated by little things, I just stop for a second and imagine how I'd feel if I lost him. That puts everything into perspective within about two seconds. I wish my parents would have learned to do that, or they might not have gotten divorced after being married more than twenty years.

One of the things I always try to do so my marriage continues to flourish is to remember to stop and consider how my attitude, words, and actions might be making my husband (as well as the other people around me) feel. I want to do all in my power to give my husband a great quality of life, just as he wants to do for me. It's so easy to become too focused on "me, me, me" and forget to put yourself in the other person's shoes. Just as the primary rule of writing is "Show, Don't Tell," I think it's the same with love.

My husband taught me this, because he's not so much a word person like I am; a word person can sometimes think that telling someone you love them is enough, but that's not going to cut it. Eric's an action guy and so, naturally, he shows his love through simple, consistent actions, like driving me to a book-signing that might be in a part of town where I don't know where I'm going. He's always looking out for me.

One time recently, while I was stressing out over a book deadline, he brought such a big smile to my face when he came home with a beautiful Gerbera daisy for me. I defy anyone to be a grouch when there's a bright pink Gerbera daisy on your desk!

Just a small thing, but every time I looked at it, I knew all over again that I'm loved.

What a wonderful experience it is to put yourself aside and make someone else the center of your universe for a while. Do that on a daily basis and, in my professional opinion as a romance writer, you will soon find yourself living in your own happily-ever-after.

Photo by Redford Photography

Gaelen Foley is the *New York Times* bestselling author of sixteen historical romances set in the elegant world of early nineteenth-century England, including *My Irresistible Earl*, coming in April 2011. To learn more about Gaelen, her novels, and the romantic Regency period in which her stories are set, visit www.GaelenFoley.com.

Linda Lael Miller

A Hero You Can Trust

To me, the essential element of romance is trust. Anything less is dysfunctional, to put it in the kindest possible way.

In my stories, I try to make my heroines as strong and independent as the heroes. They really want this guy in their life, and they love him madly, but they have goals of their own, and know they won't perish like some wilting flower if things don't work out. They'll be perfectly fine on their own. The heroes are men of integrity—however it may appear to the heroine at times—and when they commit, they mean it.

It's easy to be skeptical and say, "Well, that's just a romance novel," but in real life, the best marriages are between two strong people who are in the relationship by choice. They're willing to trust each other and ride out the rough water.

New York Times bestselling author **Linda Lael Miller** is one of today's most successful authors. With more than eighty novels to her credit, Linda writes contemporary and historical novels that have earned her awards and placements on all the national bestsellers lists. Romance Writers of America awarded her their prestigious Lifetime Achievement Award in 2007. Please visit her website at www.lindalaelmiller.com.

Jannine Corti Petska

Romance Is Calling: Don't Hang Up

Meeting my husband may not have played out like a romance novel, but finding romance comes in many different ways.

When I was eighteen, I had no clue what love was between a man and a woman. My parents weren't openly affectionate with each other. I assumed it was the same with other married couples. My girlfriends related a few details of what they did with their boyfriends. It seemed odd to me. I had been raised by Old World parents whose first language was Italian. They were much older than my friends' parents, and they sheltered me as if I were a nun.

After high school graduation, they sent me to Italy to live with my dad's brother who was a general in the Italian Air Force. He and his family lived just outside of Rome. I met my first love there, or what I thought was love. Mario had long hair, rode a motorcycle, was the drummer in a rock band, and he worked in a butcher shop. There was just one problem. My uncle had me followed by men in black suits driving a black car. Everywhere I went there they were, killing any kind of relationship with Mario. Then there were the long distance phone calls to my father, my uncle ranting about the girls in America having too much freedom. When I flew home almost two months later, my budding romance died. I was devastated in true teenage dramatic angst.

The next summer, my sister and her family took me along on their vacation just two hours south of Los Angeles to the coastal town of Oceanside. What better place to dream of romance than lying on the beach or sitting on the porch of a beach-front cottage, soaking in the rays and boy watching. I was not schooled in the matter of boys on the verge of manhood and how they behaved. It was a time of halter tops and bell bottoms. Of course, there were a few guys who tried to relieve me of my trendy clothes. I slapped each and every one of them. Needless to say, I never had a real boyfriend.

Hanging out at a popular place on the beach, I noticed a really cute guy. At the time I thought the only thing wrong with him was his lips. They seemed a bit large. My girlfriend said he was interested in me, so I figured why not? I could get past his lips. We talked and hung out together until it was time for me to head back to L.A. A few days later, we received a collect call from him. My mom said "You must have the wrong number." I asked who it was. Just before she hung up the receiver, she told me the guy's name—Ken. I jump up from my chair and shouted frantically, "Don't hang up!"

If I hadn't been at the kitchen table that day, I doubt I'd ever have seen Ken again. And if his mother hadn't been a supervisor with the phone company, he wouldn't have been able to obtain my unlisted phone number. So began our somewhat long distance romance.

The first time he drove up to see me and I introduced him to my mother, she didn't say "hi." Instead she asked, "Are you hungry?" My future husband fell in love with my mother on the spot. Being Italian, my mom cooked food for him that he hadn't ever tasted, at least not in the authentic Italian way. I used to wonder if he drove up to see me or to eat my mother's food!

When I visited him, we'd take long walks on the beach. I still remember that he never looked at another girl when he was with me. I really thought I was special. It felt like slipping on a warm, fuzzy bathrobe, the one you wrap yourself in for a cozy, comfortable and familiar feeling. He bought a gift now and then, not big expensive ones, but gifts from the heart. Our first Christmas together—four months after we'd met—my older sisters thought he would give me an engagement ring. They were giddy when they saw the wrapped jewelry box. Were they ever disappointed! In the box was a charm for my bracelet. I loved it, all the more so because Ken listened to what I had said and he remembered that I'd wanted more charms. He spent Christmas with my family, then for New Year's we drove down to where he lived.

Our New Year's Eve was quiet, just me and him. We grabbed dinner then went back to his place to ring in the New Year. At the stroke of midnight, he asked me to marry him. I was stunned, and I never said yes. He figured I rejected the idea of marriage to him and it wasn't mentioned again. I'm sure he was thinking he'd dodged a bullet. We had both been drinking, although he was the only one drunk. After I returned home, Ken got the shock of his life when he learned my sisters were planning our wedding. To this day he reminds me that I never accepted his proposal.

From the moment we said "I do," we began growing together. I was nineteen and he was twenty-one. Both of us were immature, certainly neither of us knew a thing about married life. We've had our ups and downs, but back then you didn't divorce over an argument. You stayed together and worked it out. Now, thirty-eight years later, we are still in love, a love that's grown stronger with each passing day. He is the love of my life, and I know he feels the same about me. And as I've often said, he's my knight in shining armor. Oh . . . and I definitely learned the advantage of his "big" lips.

Jannine Corti Petska, author of The Sisters of Destiny trilogy and *Rebel Heart,* was born in New York but raised in Southern California. She began writing romance novels when she was a stay-at-home mom. She tutored Italian, Spanish, German, and English as a Second Language, and loves placing stories in medieval Italy, but has also written romantic tales of the cowboy in the American West. Visit Jannine at her website at italy9@cox.net or www.jcortipetska.com.

Joan Johnston
Thoughtfulness Is the Key

I think the key to a good, long-lasting, happy relationship is thoughtfulness. I suppose that means caring what the other person wants and needs and doing your best to fulfill those needs. Sometimes that's going to be great sex. But sometimes just good sex is great enough and sometimes what you need most is cuddling. Sometimes that's going to be taking out the trash without being asked. Or attending a business dinner when you're dog-tired. Or helping put the kids to bed. Or going to a football game, even if he doesn't really like football. Or fixing a surprise dinner, just for the fun of it.

Being thoughtful allows you to get through the rough times, because if your focus is on what the other person wants and needs, you're going to allow for times when there is no sex, when the garbage doesn't get taken out, when cuddling is out of the question. Or when the full burden of shopping and cleaning and child care falls on your shoulders. Because you know that when you are down and out, the other person will pick up the slack. You're relying on your partner to be there, and he is.

I suppose that's why I write romance novels, because heroes are always thoughtful and caring. Even if they're a little prickly on the outside, the gooey stuff (the caring) is always there on the inside. With a thoughtful person sleeping on the other side of the bed, you know your partner is carrying his share of the load (and more) whenever he can, because he cares enough about you to want to lighten your burden.

Award-winning **Joan Johnston**, a lawyer by trade, has been writing for twenty-five years and has reached her goal of becoming a *New York Times* and *USA Today* bestselling author. About ten million of her books—historical, contemporary and category romance and romantic suspense—are in print, and her fiftieth novel, *Invincible*, is in bookstores now. Please visit her website at www.joanjohnston.com.

Stephanie Bond

How Do You Spell R-O-M-A-N-C-E?

What keeps romance alive and what makes it last? I believe the answer is simply being nice to each other—at least as nice as you would be to a stranger! I'm amazed at the way some couples treat each other and talk to each other day in and day out, then are surprised when they realize that romance has drained out of their relationship.

It's all about the little ways you connect every day—a pleasant "Good morning, Sweetie," a heartfelt "Have a nice day" and later asking "What was the best part of your day?" go a long way toward connecting with your lover over the long haul. Also, "please" and "thank you" are overlooked magical, romantic words! One-line e-mails when you're apart, holding hands, taking long walks together, and doing simple, fun things like going to the movies help to reinforce those daily connections.

And try to spend time alone as a couple, away from the kids, other couples, and in-laws. (Moving away from your respective families makes you rely more on each other.) And sometime throughout the year, set aside time to reevaluate your goals as a couple—financial, creative, and otherwise. Creating and sharing a Life List is a great way to explore individual and joint experiences. The only way you can grow as a partner is to continue to grow as a person. And when you find that special person, don't be afraid to love them to your full capacity. To live large, you must love large.

Stephanie Bond was a systems engineer and pursuing an MBA when an instructor remarked she had a flair for writing. With no formal training, she started writing fiction in her spare time. Now a full-time writer with more than fifty published novels, Stephanie writes a humorous mystery series called Body Movers. Please visit her website at www.stephaniebond.com.

Cheryl Brooks

He's Still the One

I've fallen in and out of love with more men than I can count, beginning with kindergarten right on up to the present day. Most of these love affairs have only been in my mind, or have at least been very one-sided, but now, I'm actually taking those daydreams and turning them into romance novels.

Despite my intense awareness of the opposite sex, until I was twenty years old, I had never had a man I could call my own. I was young and idealistic, fresh out of nursing school, but just hadn't clicked with any of the boys I knew in school. There were several that I had crushes on, but it was never mutual, and I've never really been sure why. Perhaps it was due to my inherent shyness—a lot went on in my mind, but you could never see it in my face. My actions never spoke very loudly, either. As a bit of a tomboy, I never had much use for "girly" things, and flirting was as unnatural for me as flying would be for a toad.

However, all of that changed when I got my first nursing job. I had been on day shift orientation for a couple of months following graduation in May, and so, it was late summer when I began my real job as a floor nurse on the night shift. Our hospital had male orderlies on each shift, and one of the night staff was an aging, rather colorless fellow who was more tolerated than appreciated, but then, there was Bud, the handsome, dark-haired young college student. With broad shoulders and a terrific smile, he leaned over the desk and asked if we needed help with anything.

To say it was love at first sight would be an exaggeration, but he definitely caught my eye. I wasn't alone, however; just about every female staff member in the hospital from the young aides to the battle weary RNs was already smitten. I had competition, but there were also those who thought we were made for one another. The odd thing was, for the first time, I wasn't content to let the romance play out in my head and was determined to land this one. I had help from one of the nurses I worked with who actually told him I liked him, but somehow, I think he already knew that.

I acted differently around him than I ever had before—felt happier, more alive. There was a strong sexual attraction, of course, but more than that, I actually liked him. I'd known lots of guys who were attractive, and some that I liked as friends, but I'd rarely felt both of those things for the same man. He, however, had it all, and when he asked me to a party at his sister's house, I was ecstatic. I remember the scene quite vividly: He was talking to me as he got on the elevator to go do something on another floor, and the door kept trying to close on him. When I agreed to the date, he let the door close. I'm still not sure if he heard my reaction, but it was a resounding, "YES!!!!"

We've been together for more than thirty years now. We've had our ups and downs, but we've always managed to sort things out and keep our love alive. I still fantasize about romance, just as I've always done, and though there have been times when he hasn't understood the reason for it, I think I've finally convinced him that though another handsome fellow might inspire a romance novel, he's still the one.

Cheryl Brooks is a critical care nurse by night and a romance writer by day. Her published works include *Slave, Warrior, Rogue, Outcast, Fugitive,* and *Hero*. She is a member of the RWA and lives with her husband, two sons, three horses, six cats, and one dog in rural Indiana. Please visit her website at www.cherylbrooksonline.com.

Patricia Potter

Respect Keeps Romance Alive

I think the most important factor in a romance is a deep respect for each other. Grand lust is wonderful, but it fades over time. Love remains when two people respect each other's feelings, opinions, and beliefs. When there's respect, there's consideration. When there's respect, the mate's feelings come before your own, and that magnifies the feelings of both.

One of the great love stories that fascinate me is that of Mary Matalin and James Carville. She's a Republican advocate who worked for the first President Bush. He's a Democrat activist who worked for President Clinton. She came from a wealthy East Coast family; he came from a poor Louisiana Cajun family. Though they often debate each other on national news programs, you can see the respect, trust, and love shining from each other.

Without friendship, respect, and a true appreciation of the other's feelings, you have little of lasting value. And with that respect, each does those small but wonderful things—love notes; small, inexpensive, but meaningful gifts; an "I love you" upon awakening—that keeps romance alive.

Patricia Potter is a bestselling and award-winning author of more than thirty books and six novellas. She was named Story Teller of the Year in 1993 by Romantic Times, and received the magazine's 1995 Career Achievement Award for Western Romances. She has been published in fifteen countries and has frequently been on the *USA Today* and Waldenbooks Bestseller list. Pat lives in Memphis, Tennessee, with two insecure Shelties and a know-it-all toy poodle. Please view her website at www.patriciapotter.com.

Sharon Lathan

My Own Mr. Darcy

I like to tease that my husband picked me up while hanging out on the Boardwalk. Sounds juicier somehow and I love the raised eyebrows! The fact is that while technically true that we met on the boardwalk fronting the sandy beaches of Santa Cruz, California, our meeting was innocent and not particularly exciting.

It was my very first day in town. Although July, I was newly relocated from New Mexico where the temperature at midnight is still in the 80s. My best friend insisted on showing me the famous sights of the town while all I wanted to do was curl up under the heating blanket set on super-high. How was I to know an enchanted moment was to occur? At least it was enchanting for my future soul mate. To this day I am not sure if my memories of being introduced to him are actually his vividly retold remembrances of the encounter or mine. I only recall shivering in the fog and vaguely meeting a friend of my friend. My husband recalls every detail, including the clothes I was wearing! Guess which of us is the romantic in this relationship? That's right, not the romance writer!

Yet even without shooting fireworks or slow-motion fading of peripheral images, it was a momentous happenstance and exactly one year and two days later we were married. We were the epitome of the happy couple deliriously in love, with me the blushing bride in white and him the handsome groom nervously reciting his lines.

Twenty-four years later, I remember the flutters and wild passion of new love—just not that day on the Boardwalk! But I also know the profound bonding that comes from years together. I now understand that romance is roses and candlelight dinners, and that it is also caring for your loved ones when they are sick and forgiving them after an argument. I can tell you that after many years my lover's kiss still excites me and that passion is alive and well! I also know how blissful it is to sit side-by-side and watch TV or dine with the family. He is my Mr. Darcy!

Love is an emotion expressed in a myriad of ways. Love is also a conscious commitment reaffirmed every day. Trials and tribulations have taught me that. God has taught me that. And hopefully, through my stories of marriage I can teach others these principles and restore hope in the belief that love does not have to wither and romance can survive. You, too, can find your Mr. Darcy.

Photo by Steve Lathan

Sharon Lathan is the bestselling novelist of the Darcy Saga sequel series to *Jane Austen's Pride and Prejudice*. She's currently working on her next book in this series. When not writing, Sharon is a wife, mother, and twenty-five-year veteran registered nurse in neonatal intensive care. She lives with her family in the San Joaquin Valley of California at the base of the High Sierras. Visit Sharon at: www.sharonlathan.net and her group blogs: www.austenauthors.com.

Judith Arnold
Three Thousand Miles

I met Ted the day we both moved into the Graduate Towers, a blocky brick campus residence for graduate students at Brown University in Providence, Rhode Island. He was beginning doctoral work in chemistry and I was there to study creative writing. We kept running into each other, and after a week he asked me to see *Blazing Saddles* with him.

For two years we were inseparable. However, I was in a master's program, and in the spring of my second year, about a month before I would receive my degree, I was offered a university teaching job in California. I didn't want to leave him, but we both knew that if I turned down a desirable job to remain with him while he finished his Ph.D., I would resent him forever. If our love could survive a three-thousand-mile separation, we'd know it was the real thing. If it couldn't survive, so be it.

That summer, I moved across the country to California. I wrote weepy, sappy poetry about missing him. I struggled to adjust to the culture of the "Left Coast." I lived my life and he lived his. We had no e-mail in those days, no text messaging, no Facebook or Skype. We were two kids on tight budgets; we could barely afford long-distance phone calls. And gradually we drifted as far apart emotionally as we were physically.

When I flew to New York that winter to spend the holidays with my parents, he drove to the city to see me. I told him I thought we ought to break up. Since he was already dating someone else, he agreed that we should make the break-up official.

At the end of the holiday, I flew back to California. I developed a sharp pain in my leg on the flight back, and by the time I returned to my apartment I could barely walk. I was twenty-three years old, living thousands of miles away from family and friends. I found a doctor, made an appointment, and received a scary diagnosis.

Ted surprised me a couple of days later by phoning—just to see if I was okay. Maybe he'd gotten a premonition or an intuition. Maybe he was just testing me to make sure the break-up was for real. But I blurted out that I was sick, and he said, "I'm coming."

Abandoning his research, buying a plane ticket with money he didn't have and flying across the country—his first time in an airplane—was a huge gesture. But he told me he was worried and didn't want me to be alone while I dealt with this medical problem. The hell with our break-up—he had to be with me.

He stayed for two weeks. I got better. And by the end of those two weeks, I knew what love was: not roses, not flowery poetry, not wine and chocolate, not hot sex (although all those things can certainly make love even better), but caring so much about another person that you will fly three thousand miles across the country to make sure that person is all right. You will rush to her side when she's afraid, and take care of her, and see her through a crisis.

A year and a half later, I quit my teaching job and moved back east. Two years after that, we got married. Thirty years later . . . we're still married.

The author of more than eighty-five novels, **Judith Arnold** has won awards from RT Book Reviews for Best Harlequin American Romance, Best Harlequin Superromance, Best Series Romance, and Best Contemporary Romance. *Publishers Weekly* named her novel *Love in Bloom's* one of the best books of the year. Her current release is *Meet Me in Manhattan*. Please visit her website at www.juditharnold.com.

Karen Robards
For the Long Haul

I met my husband when I was seventeen years old. I was a wide-eyed college freshman, and he was a senior—big man on campus, in my view at least. My roommate, Peggy, and I had stopped by a Dairy Queen, and we were sitting at the counter getting ready to eat the sundaes we had ordered when a male voice behind us said, "That looks good. Can I have a bite?" We turned around to find these two good-looking guys. Peggy (the more outgoing of the pair of us) offered up a bite of her sundae, and the dark-haired guy ate it. Then he asked if he could give us a ride back to our dorm. (Freshmen weren't allowed to have cars on campus.) We agreed, he and his friend drove us home, and—well, dear readers, five years later I married him.

Thirty-two years after that first meeting, we've had three sons, whom we are still in the process of raising together. We've bought three houses and a farm, and renovated all of them. We've had good times and hard times, lost family members and gained others. We've changed physically—he's lost some hair, I've gained some weight. We've had lots of fights, and done lots of making up. But sometimes, when I see him walking toward me, I still see that good-looking dark-haired young jock I fell in love with.

The bottom line is, we're both in it for the long haul: until death (or murder) does us part. And to me, that's romance.

Karen Robards is the author of more than forty books and one novella. She is the mother of three boys and lives in her hometown of Louisville, Kentucky. A regular on the *New York Times, USA Today,* and *Publishers Weekly* bestseller lists, among others, she published her first novel at age twenty-four. "I read, I write, and I chauffeur children," she says with a laugh. "That's my life." Please visit her website at www.karenrobards.com.

Suzanne Forster

Who's the Boss?

The way my husband and I met would make a great old-fashioned boss/secretary romance! I was a young divorced mom back in those days, raising my toddler and toiling eight to five in the Aerospace industry. I still have vivid memories of having my purse searched by security guards at check-in and then racing to beat the time clock. Time cards had to be punched by 8 AM on the dot in order not to have your pay docked. It was rather prisonlike, to be honest, but the pay was better than other clerical jobs.

I was interviewed for the position by the division director, a kindly balding man who was married with a passel of kids. I thought I'd be working for him, but when I reported in, I was assigned to "Mr. Forster," a project engineer who was away on business.

I don't know what I was expecting, but it wasn't the dark-haired, dark-eyed Adonis in his early thirties who showed up the next morning, carrying a Styrofoam cup of coffee and a warm smile, both of which were for me.

He wasn't kindly, balding, or married with a passel of kids. "Mr. Forster" was single, very eligible, and he was my boss. I spent the next year being wildly attracted to him. Who wouldn't have? I swear, they could justifiably blame global warming on that smile. He also had a disconcerting way of looking deeply into your eyes and making you forget that anyone else existed. You've all heard that one, right? Well, I'm here to tell you it isn't just another romantic cliché. He still kids me about the time he stopped at my desk to speak with me about something and he had to pick up the phone because I didn't hear it ringing. Apparently it rang several times, enough to make him wonder if I had a hearing problem.

Difficult as it might be to believe, I really did make every effort to hide my feelings for him because anything else would have been inappropriate. Our mutual employer was one of the largest aerospace firms in the country and there were rules about fraternization.

We followed the rules to the letter, of course, but that doesn't mean I wasn't fraternizing in my heart. Every morning that he wasn't traveling, we would meet in his office and map out the day ahead. He liked to dictate rather than use machines and it was amazing how intimate something as perfunctory as dictation could be, under those circumstances. Even normal business terms took on special meaning: "I look forward to a long and rewarding association." "I know we can do great things together." "Please respond as soon as possible." "I await your call." "'Very truly yours. . . ."

Very truly mine? Oh, my beating heart! I had to steady my hand and concentrate or I knew I'd never be able to read what I'd written.

When I was feeling brave, I would think of reasons to stay in the charged zone of his office, asking questions about the work and secretly hoping that our conversation might turn personal, as it occasionally did. I had pictures of my two-year-old son on my desk and at least once a week, he would ask how Kenny and I were faring on our own in southern California. I'd relocated from Washington State to leave a bad situation behind and move on with my life, so I deeply appreciated his interest, but never allowed myself to think he was being anything more than polite.

Of course, I thought I had everything under control, but I was kidding myself. One fateful afternoon, I discovered that I had a rival for "Mr. Forster's" affections! My boss was coming out of the division director's office and he stopped to talk to the director's beautiful blond secretary. They laughed and joked and flirted, or at least it appeared that way to me, especially since I knew she was single and available. What would he want with me when he could have a gorgeous creature like her? I brought with me a ready-made family and how many men wanted to take that on?

Ah, the anguish! The beautiful blond was a perfectly nice person, but that didn't faze me. In the days and weeks that followed, I began to search for flaws in her appearance and wish bad hair days on her. Eventually my angst became such a distraction that I decided to transfer out of the group. I made the move while the object of my anguish—my boss—was gone on an extended assignment in Washington DC and I never said a word to him. I put in for a transfer, interviewed with another group, and left.

The new group was in another building, which might as well have been another world. I never expected to see "Mr. Forster" again, so imagine my shock when he showed up in the cafeteria one day, about a month later, and asked in front of all my friends if I would join him for lunch. I thought he might be angry at the way I left and I tried to apologize, but he wouldn't let me. He just wanted to talk, to catch up. He'd missed me. Missed me?

The cafeteria wasn't exactly a romantic spot and we were objects of intense scrutiny, but it was the giddiest, most memorable lunch of my life. Please, don't anyone ask me what I ate. No clue.

We began to date after that. Since I wasn't working for him there were no issues of fraternization. Actually, we began to date a lot. It was intense right from the beginning, probably because of all those months of anticipation! But it wasn't easy carrying on a romance and being a single working mom. My son needed my time and attention. Fortunately, Allan understood that completely. He made it a point to include Kenny on what he called "family dates" and we planned nearly every weekend around my son. When Allan and I went out, he insisted on paying for the babysitter, so that our relationship wouldn't be an emotional or financial burden for me.

Clearly, this guy was a gem. He wasn't like any other man I'd ever known, so it shouldn't have been a surprise that his proposal of marriage was unique as well. Shortly after we started dating, I introduced him to jogging and we were on a high school track one Saturday afternoon, collapsed on the grass after running a record two miles. I was hot and sweaty and struggling to catch my breath.

Suddenly the breathing got a lot harder. Allan produced a small black velvet ring box and began telling me how much I meant to him. I couldn't believe he'd chosen that moment, when

I was looking—and feeling—so grungy. What girl doesn't want to look pretty when her guy pops the question! I should have known he would have a good reason. More than once I had confessed to him that he was so darn cute he made me insecure about my looks, and he was smart enough to realize I wasn't kidding. By proposing when I looked like a rung-out dishrag, he was reassuring me that he loved me for reasons that had nothing to do with my looks. He said it was my energy, my passion, and my goodness that he loved—and he actually used the word goodness. That was when I realized that handsome as he was, his most attractive feature by far was his character.

Now, all these years later, I'm still insecure—and he still makes me feel like the prettiest girl at the party. What a gift that is. As for him, he can still turn on his amazing smile and heat-seeking gaze. But as often happens with long-married couples, we've done a little role-reversing over the years. Oh, sure, every once in awhile I call him the boss just to watch him preen. But guess who makes the decisions these days? And guess who made a most excellent decision all those years ago when she said yes to a sweaty young Adonis on a high school track? Mrs. Forster, that's who.

New York Times and *USA Today* bestselling author **Suzanne Forster** has written more than forty novels and been the recipient of countless awards, including the National Readers Choice Award. Suzanne has a master's degree in writing popular fiction and teaches and lectures frequently. She lives in Newport Beach, California, and can be contacted through her website at www.suzanneforster.com.

Karen White

A Match Made at Wimbledon

This year marks my twenty-third wedding anniversary. Not bad, considering my husband and I had never lived in the same state—or country—before we got married. No, it wasn't something as exotic as an arranged marriage, or even a love-at-first-sight story. It had a lot more to do with my belief in the old adage of choosing a man to marry based on how he treats his sister and mother. Having been raised with three brothers, now all married, it's painfully obvious to me that most women ignore this advice. But I digress.

When I was twelve years old, my father's job took us to London, England, where I lived until I graduated from the American School in London and started college. But in my junior year in high school a new girl, Claire White, moved from Pennsylvania in the middle of the year. She joined my chemistry class and was assigned as my lab partner. We clicked and became best friends, despite the fact that on that first day I thought she was a student teacher, and she thought I was an idiot because I left her with her hand stuck inside a glass tube (I think we were fermenting or distilling *something*) to go get help and was sidetracked by my need to socialize.

My family lived in the city of London, on Regent's Park, but her family had a lovely penthouse condo in the town of Wimbledon, their living room windows overlooking Centre Court of the famous tennis arena. We took turns spending weekends at each other's houses, and talking about our families—especially since both of us had two older brothers already in college (although I had a younger brother still at home). Claire was always telling me about her two older brothers, Mick and Tim. I was especially interested in Mick because he was a cadet at West Point. However, I was still excited when Claire told me that Tim was going to be visiting that summer. Our first meeting took place in the lines waiting to get inside the Wimbledon Tennis Tournament. Tim had an ROTC crew cut and a beard. The fact that he'd spent the night in the ticket line did nothing to enhance his appearance. Needless to say, it wasn't love at first sight.

Our second meeting later that day didn't improve matters. For some reason that still escapes me, I was in the White's living room lip-syncing to Meatloaf's "Paradise by the Dashboard Light," and Tim walked in just as I was throwing myself onto their sofa—the one with wheels and parked on the wood floors—and just in time to see me propel myself across the room and into the opposing wall. He wasn't impressed.

Following high school graduation, Claire and I kept in touch, even though Claire's family was back home in Pennsylvania and my family had moved to the Netherlands. But every school break I visited at the Whites' house. Tim was there often and we quickly became sparring partners with our banter going back and forth until Claire had to break us up. However, that was just our way of letting it be known that we liked each other without coming right out and saying it.

When I was a senior in college and visiting the Whites at Christmas, Tim mentioned that his company was hosting a black tie formal awards dinner at the Waldorf Astoria in New York and that he needed a date. At my request, Claire told her brother that her friend wanted to go with him.

After that first date, Tim and I commuted back and forth between Baltimore where he was living and New Orleans, where I was a senior at Tulane University. Upon graduation, I found a job in Washington DC to be near Tim. The first day at work, Tim told me that he'd been transferred to Philadelphia.

Within six months, we were engaged. To this day, Tim sticks to his claim that he proposed only to corral our traveling expenses and phone bills.

Claire, as the instigator in our relationship, was maid of honor at our wedding and is also the godmother of our two children. We're still best friends, and enjoy vacationing together with both our families. We've even talked about retiring in houses next door to each other since she and I have never lived close by except for that one year in high school.

And, despite hours of tennis lessons, tennis teams, and tennis matches, it doesn't appear as if either one of our children will end up where it all began—at Wimbledon.

New York Times bestselling author **Karen White** currently writes what she refers to as *grit lit*—southern women's fiction—as well as a mystery series set in Charleston. Her fourteenth novel, *Falling Home*, was published in November 2010 and she is currently contracted with Penguin for three more books. Visit her website at www.karen-white.com or e-mail her at AuthorKarenWhite@aol.com.

Secret Key #7

Hope

WHEN YOU WRITE ROMANCE, YOU HAVE TO PUT IN THE GRAND, SWEEPING GESTURES AND THE PASSIONATE DECLARATIONS, BUT IN REAL LIFE, TRUE LOVE SNEAKS UP ON YOU, CATCHES YOU WHEN YOU'RE NOT LOOKING, AND TEACHES YOU THINGS YOU DIDN'T EVEN KNOW YOU NEEDED TO LEARN.

–*Laura Lee Guhrke*

Jane Porter

Forty and Fabulous

At forty I found myself unexpectedly single. I'd never planned to be divorced, or a single mother to two boys. I was floored. Make that devastated.

In April, just two months after my fortieth birthday, I went to Hawaii on the spur of the moment to finish a book for my London publisher. I was newly separated and finding it difficult to write in Seattle since my boys were with their dad for Easter. Only I wasn't happier in Hawaii. I just felt sadder. The five star hotel was beautiful, the ocean sparkled, the wind rustled the palm fronds outside my window, but I missed my children. I missed my old life. I missed everything that had once defined me.

For a week I struggled to focus, struggled to imagine a future where I'd see my children only part time, struggled to believe that anyone could love a battered, bruised me. But as the days passed all those intense emotions raised questions, questions I thought could maybe drive a new story: What happens to women as they become wives and mothers? What happens to our sense of humor and sense of self? Why do we become afraid of change and new things? I drew on everything around me—my divorce, my sense of loss, my confusion at being single, as well the fancy hotel, and the sexy surfer who strolled through the pool area one afternoon. Within two days I had plotted a whole new book—the beginning, middle, and end.

Once I sat down to write the book, I wrote it in a matter of months. I knew the story so well. I knew what I wanted to say and this is a book that almost wrote itself. Maybe this is part of the story's power. I was honest. I was raw. I was determined there would be a happy ending, too. The novel did have a happy ending. It became my bestselling novel, *Flirting with Forty*, and was turned into a Lifetime movie starring Heather Locklear in December of 2008.

But something else happened while writing this story. Life and fiction collided. I began dating the sexy surfer after interviewing him, and in the following months, I started flying to Hawaii whenever I could. Things got serious and within two years we'd bought a home together in Hawaii, not far from where Ty taught surfing in Waikiki. It's been nearly eight years and Ty still teaches surfing in Waikiki, and I'm still writing romance novels, but we're now parents to a busy, happy surf baby and enjoying our chaotic surfer/writer life.

To this day, people think I wrote about my life, but at the time I pitched the story to my editor, it was just a plot. A concept. Yet here we are proving that romance novel endings do come true.

But our relationship wouldn't have been possible if there hadn't been that spark of hope and flicker of possibility—what if a handsome young surf instructor fell in love with a soccer mom? What if he loved her despite her stretch marks, wrinkles, and those few extra pounds?

While *Flirting with Forty* helped me imagine a new

beginning, it was Surfer Ty who taught me that forty-year-old soccer moms are beautiful.

I love a happy ending. But then, I think we all do.

Jane Porter, bestselling author of thirty novels, has been a four-time finalist for the prestigious RITA award from Romance Writers of America. Jane's book *Flirting With Forty*, picked by *Redbook* as its Red Hot Summer Read, went back for seven printings in six weeks before being made into a December 2008 Lifetime movie starring Heather Locklear. Jane's newest release is *She's Gone Country*. A busy mother of three sons, Jane holds a master's degree in writing from the University of San Francisco and makes her home in Bellevue, Washington. Please visit her website at www.janeporter.com.

Dee Davis
True Love

My mother spent the night with my father in the first grade. Daddy asked Mama if she could stay over and their parents realized they either had to explain the facts of life to six year olds or simply allow my mother and dad to have a sleepover. They've been together ever since. In the third grade, my dad gave my mother his Boy Scout ring, which she promptly lost, and found again after diligently retracing her path home that day. We still have that ring somewhere.

The romance continued through high school until their parents convinced them to break up when my dad went away to college. They've both separately admitted that it was a very long summer. But when my mom arrived at the University of Oklahoma they were quickly reunited.

Theirs was the kind of great romance we read about and wonder if it truly exists. When people used my parents' names, they were spoken as one word—"SusieandRonnie." And though we had a wonderful family life, there was always time carved out for just the two of them. Most memorably the hour or so between when my father came home from work and when we sat down for dinner. My brother and I were banned from the kitchen. And in our eyes at least, it seemed a magical time. Two people who took time to shut out the entire world so that it was just the two of them.

In short, I grew up watching true love up close and personal. Until the day my father died, they were intrinsically bound together, two parts of a whole. And I was lucky to be in their orbit.

But living in the presence of that kind of love can be daunting when it comes to finding it yourself. I knew with all of my heart that I couldn't settle for anything less than what Mama and Daddy had, and yet I also knew that it was a rare thing, this kind of love, and that it might not happen for me. I was especially concerned because at a young age I believed that, like my mother, I needed to meet the man of my dreams in first grade. Only we moved every two years and so if I did indeed meet him, I never got the chance to build that relationship.

In fact, moving as often as I did, I didn't get to develop much in the way of relationships at all. Just as I began to think maybe I'd found a boy I could grow to love it was time to move again, and without the instant connections of today's world, he was pretty much lost to me forever. A few wistful angsty letters and then he was part of my past.

Then once I was settled enough, in college and later as I built a career, I found that finding Mr. Right wasn't as easy as my parents' story made it seem. In short, I had to kiss a lot of frogs before I found a prince. But the same mother who loved my father, also loved me. And she was quick to remind me that perseverance is the name of the game.

So even when my brother found the love of his life and all of my relatives were tittering about his unmarried older sister, I remained strong, still convinced that my Mr. Right was out there. All I had to do was have a little faith—and dump my long-term, never going to commit boyfriend. Now before you start feeling sorry for me, let me hasten to say that I had a lovely time with lots of almost prince charmings. Several of whom I still hold dear today.

And besides, this story has a happy ending. Just when I'd given up all hope (and isn't that always when we find the most amazing things), I found him. On a blind date that I didn't even realize was a set-up. It sailed right over my head when a dear friend introduced me to a colleague of hers from work while I was visiting her from out of town. And I missed the significance again when she proceeded to insist that we go to dinner with him and another of their friends.

I wasn't looking for love. I was too busy licking my wounds and trying to recover from the fact that the ex-boyfriend who'd said he couldn't commit had actually meant "to me," and had walked down the aisle with someone else just over three months after we'd split. In fact, I wasn't certain I was capable of falling in love at all—until I heard Robert laugh. It's the kind of sound that isn't describable. Not even by a writer. But it's so full of joy and abandonment that it makes you smile no matter your mood.

And so, after our not-blind date, with much encouragement from aforementioned friend, I worked up my courage and asked him to come with me to a golf tournament. Even bought a new outfit to wear. But it rained and I figured our chances had fizzled before they had the chance to start. And then he called and asked me to lunch instead. Afterward, the rain having cleared to a brilliant blue sky, we went on to the golf tournament. He was witty and charming and we shared our first kiss. And in an instant I recognized that this was it. This was "the one."

We had four dates that weekend while I was in Austin. And then I went home and bought an answering machine. I'd always hated the idea of being held hostage by the telephone, and so had refused to give into the trend, but suddenly I realized that missing his call was something I feared even more. It took three very long days, but eventually the phone rang and the rest is history.

Exactly one year after we kissed at that golf tournament, he asked me to marry him. On the sixteenth hole. I never did find out who won the tournament, but I did find my own happy ending. And it was worth the wait, because twenty years later I still hear that laugh and look up to see him smiling across the room at me and know that all is right with my world. I'm one of the lucky ones. Just like my mother and father, I found true love.

Award-winning author **Dee Davis** worked in public relations before turning her hand to writing. She is the author of eighteen books and three novellas, including the A-Tac series. When not frantically trying to meet a deadline, Dee spends her time with her husband, daughter, cat, and Cardigan Welsh corgi. Please visit Dee at www.deedavis.com.

Robin Lee Hatcher

A More Excellent Way

Ah, love. Writers of romance believe in it with all their hearts. I know I do. I love to write stories about two unlikely people finding their way to each other, discovering a new future because two have become one. Romance is about hope for the future and a life made better because two people are walking the path together.

But we live in a society that all-too-seldom considers the cost of true love—and there is a cost to loving another human being. It isn't easy, whether that be the love of a man for a woman or a mother for a child or even a friend for a friend. Loving someone opens us up to hurt and disappointment as well as unspeakable joy.

Love is a verb, not a feeling. It's an action. Anyone can say the words, "I love you." Yet those are meaningless words unless the actions of love follow them. Love is what you do when the other person is unlovable. It's putting the other person's needs above your own. True love is sacrificial and abiding and worth striving for.

I don't believe there is any better description of real love than the beautiful verses from 1 Corinthians 13 that have been used in countless wedding ceremonies through the decades:

Love is patient and kind. Love is not jealous or boastful or proud or rude. It does not demand its own way. It is not irritable, and it keeps no record of being wronged. It does not rejoice about injustice but rejoices whenever the truth wins out. Love never gives up, never loses faith, is always hopeful, and endures through every circumstance.

I have loved deeply in my life, and I have mourned the loss of love as well. But I continue to believe that, love is the more excellent way.

Robin Lee Hatcher is the bestselling author of more than sixty books. Her well-drawn characters and heartwarming stories of faith, courage, and love have earned her both critical acclaim and the devotion of readers. Robin's numerous awards include two RITA Awards for Inspirational Romance, the Christy Award for Excellence in Christian Fiction, the National Readers Choice Award, and the RWA Lifetime Achievement Award. She makes her home in Idaho, sharing it with Poppet, the high-maintenance Papillon. Please visit her website at www.robinleehatcher.com.

Jade Lee
The Walk to the Roof

Markley dormitory has six floors plus a roof. I had made it up to the fourth and was trying to steel my nerve to go to the top. The jump to the cement pavement below would surely end my life and the unrelenting emptiness that defined me.

It is not that my life was so awful. In fact, to many I had it all. I was the daughter of two wealthy, highly intelligent, and motivated people. Raised to be one of the best and the brightest, I was given the best genes, the best work ethic, and the best education with which to shine. At eighteen, I was beginning what should become a stellar life.

Too bad I had no idea where or how I wanted to shine.

How could I be a star if nothing interested me? The least little spark of curiosity led to a sudden and immediate need to perform better than anyone else. I couldn't just draw, I had to be an artist. I couldn't read about another culture, I had to become a diplomat. I couldn't be a child, I was in training to become the first woman president or a concert pianist or a Supreme Court judge.

I had all the tools—including the self-discipline needed to succeed—but no love for any task or goal. Everything I did, from going to school to learning how to drive, became tedious. The thought of a lifetime of such drudgery was more than I could bear.

So I climbed, aiming for the roof, and then the pavement below.

On the fourth story landing, I stopped. It was just a pause, maybe to catch my breath or steel myself for the next staircase. But in that moment, I did something I'd never done before. I spoke clearly and simply to God as if He were right beside me. There was no preamble, just a simple statement.

"Do something now or we're going to be speaking face to face."

Then I waited for a response, not really expecting anything, but being polite nonetheless.

Meanwhile, a young man on the third floor was also speaking with God, asking for help with his plan. David was shy, quiet, and very lonely. He had decided, in his practical, honest way, that he wanted a girlfriend. His plan was to ask a girl for a date.

He had already chosen who he wanted. She was pretty, vivacious, and always surrounded by friends. He never guessed that at eighteen she had yet to be asked out on a date or that she worked hard at being an entertainer for the people around her because she couldn't bear to be alone. All he knew was that he liked her legs and her smile, and that he was incredibly nervous about calling her up.

I had my foot on the first step to the fifth floor when the phone rang. My roommate had to run down the hall and call through the stairwell to find me.

Though I hesitated, my curiosity got the better of me. Who could be phoning me? And why?

I turned around and answered the call.

We now have two beautiful children and a good home with

friends and family nearby. I still feel the heavy weight of failure at times, but Dave has been with me from that first moment I picked up the phone.

I thank God for David, and maybe one day, I'll even believe that failure comes only when I stop trying. My career as a bestselling novelist has been up and down since I sold *Devil's Bargain,* but that's the nature of the beast in this profession. I continue to write even when the chips are down and have discovered a love of life I never expected. . . .

Thanks to answered prayers and the love of a very good man.

A *USA Today* bestseller, **Jade Lee** "has made her mark with sizzling romances whose unique settings, intriguing backdrops and exotic characters lure you in." (Romantic Times Book Club reviews). Her China-set historical romances are a first in genre history. But she hasn't forgotten her Regency roots. Look for her new sexy historical *Wicked Surrender*. Jade also writes for Harlequin Blaze as Kathy Lyons. Please visit her at www.jadeleeauthor.com.

Haywood Smith

The Greatest Love

I've loved a lot in my life. First, I had two parents who showed me what it meant to love, and taught me I could do anything I set my mind to. My great grandmother Hansell and my father's mother, Granny Bess, were fabulous grandmothers who taught me how to make even the smallest things special.

I remember leaving our infant son with my husband's mother (who lived across the street from us). She took him into her arms and settled into a comfortable club chair, telling us to have fun on our first night out since the baby came. When we got home, she was still exactly where we'd left her, looking in adoration at our sleeping child. At the time, I thought that was really strange. Now that I have grandchildren, I understand.

I have held my sleeping grandson till my arms went numb, but I didn't want to put him down. Just holding him close, watching him breathe, inhaling the clean, innocent scent of his hair was the most fascinating thing I'd ever experienced. When his sister came along, my son and his family were far away, so I didn't get to share her first six months.

When my grandchildren come to "GoGo's," I let them set the agenda. First, we always start with a snack, which can be anything from an Oreo to fresh fruit to cold condensed alphabet soup from the can (a favorite concoction I came up with out of desperation). Then we move to the living room, where everything comes out, but I don't care. I can clean up after they're gone. After an elaborate pretend meal, we play dress-up in their room, filled with books and toys. While the kids do home repairs with their toy tools or play knights with their sponge swords and shields, we add in a book or two. Then, if the weather's nice, we go outside to pet the cats and ride trikes, or pick flowers from GoGo's garden—all the flowers they want.

Such simple things, but what a joy to share them. What a privilege to be able to drop everything and make life special for each of my grandchildren, the way my grandmothers did for me.

I respect my son and his wife's rules for the kids, but at GoGo's house, there's rarely a need for discipline. I have the luxury of distracting them, instead. I'm not the responsible parent who has to resolve power plays and mete out punishment. I'm the one who can love unconditionally, and get that love back, packed down and running over.

The greatest love I've ever known is what I feel when my grandchildren's faces light up when they see me, and when I hear them call my name and run to me, arms wide. It's the satisfaction of having my granddaughter insist I come along on their camping trip with my ex and his wife "because we'll miss you so much if you don't come."

My grandchildren are the most fun I've ever experienced—God's reward for surviving my son's adolescence. I don't know what will happen when they grow up, but I do know one thing: GoGo's house will always be the place they can come for love by the bushel, and it goes both ways.

New York Times bestselling author **Haywood Smith** has won critical acclaim and numerous awards for her six historical novels and five contemporary Southern women's humor novels. "Life gives you grief for free," Haywood says. "If you buy one of my books, you're going to enjoy the read and feel good at the end." Haywood is currently working on her next novel. Please visit her website at www.haywoodsmith.net.

Terry Spear
The Elements of Love

I write medieval and urban fantasy romances, which all have one thing in common—the happily ever after—the commitment of a couple through love, romance, and passion. For me, it's just as likely the heroine is rescuing the hero as in the other way around.

My werewolf tales are based on real wolf behaviors and one of the "conditions" is the wolf's instinct to mate for life. That's how I envision a romantic relationship that goes from the courtship phase to unconditional love—forever.

In each of my stories, the heroine is capable and very much independent. Yet having that special someone in her life—the element of romance—makes her world complete.

What constitutes romance? The encouragement, the nurturing, the respect, the little things in life that say "I love you" in a special and caring way.

What is romantic? A husband, who doesn't care for Mexican food, takes his wife to a Mexican restaurant to see her all time favorite star—Elvis Presley—or at least his impersonator, in a special show, after not wanting to be married in an Elvis wedding chapel in Las Vegas years earlier.

He's a hero in my book.

Through experience, I've learned romance encompasses the small everyday gestures that say that the man or woman in the relationship is special with no thought of reward or compensation in return. It's all about commitment to one another through the good times and bad. It's about showing the love, rather than just saying "I love you."

I've also learned I can never have enough romance in my life.

Terry Spear is an award-winning author of urban fantasy and medieval historical romantic suspense. *Heart of the Wolf* was named in *Publishers Weekly*'s Best Books of the Year. She also writes true stories for adult and young adult audiences. When she's not writing about heroic men and women, she's teaching online writing courses. Ms. Spear lives in the heart of Texas. Please visit her website at www.terryspear.com.

Leigh Greenwood
Worth the Effort

Okay, let's get the hard stuff out of the way right up front. Leigh is a man! I know men aren't supposed to write romance, but I do and I don't intend to quit. It's fun.

If you're still upset, you can blame it on my wife. I wouldn't have known what romance was if, after I got married in 1972, romances hadn't started collecting all over the house. They were everywhere I looked, in the den, on the kitchen table, in the living room, stacked along one whole wall in the bedroom, even in the bathroom. When my wife wasn't cooking or taking care of the children, she was reading a romance. I admit I was a little supercilious about her choice of reading material. After all, I was reading Dickens, Hemingway, Austen, the classics! I started calling them her "sin, lust, and passion" books. I said it so often my daughter started calling them Mommy's "celeste" passion books. I thought it was funny. My wife didn't. One day, after what I'm certain was a typically condescending remark (you have to understand I'd never read a romance, just looked at the covers and made a snap judgment), she threw a book at me and told me to read it or shut up.

Being an obedient husband (my wife's expletive deleted!), I read the book. It was Georgette Heyer's *These Old Shades*. I loved it. To this day it's one of my favorite books. I searched bookstores until I'd collected every book Georgette Heyer had ever written. Being thoroughly hooked, I asked my wife to suggest some other books. Since I have a minor in history, she started me on a diet of the icons of early historical romance, Kathleen Woodiwiss, Rosemary Rogers, Jennifer Blake, Bertrice Small, and Johanna Lindsey. By now I was completely addicted.

Somewhere along the line, I read that women could make decent money (more than I could as a music teacher) writing historicals, so I tried to get my wife to write one. She told me she couldn't write, that I ought to write one. I said I couldn't think of a plot. This went back and forth for some time until I said if she'd give me a plot, I'd write a book. She said, "I've lost everything." It wasn't a plot, but it must have been enough. I sat down and started writing. Eight hundred eighty-nine pages later, I had finished my first romance, badly overwritten, but a book nonetheless.

I didn't know much about writing, and nothing at all about the romance market, so I had to write two more books and join Romance Writers of America before I knew enough to sell my first book. *Wyoming Wildfire* was published by Zebra in 1987. Since then I've written forty-five more books and four novellas.

Unfortunately, after thirty-six years of marriage, my wife and I divorced. Not even a divorce that's necessary and amicable comes without loss. You're suddenly separated from the person you slept next to for nearly four decades, with whom you reared children and made plans for the future. House-hunting and moving from a home I'd occupied for twenty-seven years was difficult at times, but change can bring good surprises. My ex-wife is an excellent cook so I gave up cooking once we were married. Now I find that not only do I enjoy it, I'm good at it. Too often I find myself standing over a simmering sauce or making soup when I should be writing.

The lessons didn't stop there. I learned a person can be kind and forgiving even when they're hurting. I learned that the support of friends is more valuable than I ever imagined. Finally, I learned love isn't easy the second time, but it's worth the effort when you get it right.

Leigh Greenwood is the author of nearly fifty books. Among those are three western series, *Seven Brides*, *The Cowboys*, and *The Night Riders*. Leigh lives in Charlotte, North Carolina, and is the proud father of three grown children. Visit Leigh's website at www.LeighGreenwood.com, or write to leighgwood@aol.com.

Christie Ridgway

Picture This

You couldn't blame me and the man I married for at first not believing in the "ever after" that's supposed to follow "happy." Shortly after we met during college, I was blindsided by my parents' divorce. At twelve, he had lost his father to a sudden heart attack. What did long-term commitment look like? We didn't have a picture of it to hold. But we started building an album of love despite our fears. I can page through it today and see how my hope was restored and my faith in us was built.

First, there's this photo of me, a skinny college sophomore. This guy who was my brand-new boyfriend invited me along on a boys' waterskiing trip. Hey, I was a good sport (though without innate athletic ability). We got up at o'dark early, and drove to a boat docked at a nearby lake. Late October in central California was experiencing unusual cold. A shallow pool on the boat cover had iced over. With gentlemanly courtesy, they let me make the first attempt at skiing, since I was borrowing a wetsuit from the smallest of the other skiers. Yeah, it was dry, but belonged to a dude (literally—his nickname was Dude!) who was a foot taller than me and who outweighed me by fifty pounds. In the picture, my arms and legs are sticking out of the neoprene like toothpicks from rigatoni noodles. But as cautious as I had become about romance, I jumped into that chilly, chilly water because I was falling for my guy just that much.

Turn the page, and there's another image of an important moment. The first Christmas at my childhood home without my father present. Mom and I welcomed my boyfriend with relief. It gave us a reason to resume all our family traditions. The tree was beautiful, the cinnamon rolls tasty, the dinner with my aunt and uncle and cousins as full of fun and laughter as it had been in the past. My guy charmed the relatives. He reached things on high shelves. His nimble fingers played Christmas carols on our piano. Just by being the good-natured, good-hearted person he was, he made the holiday feel like a celebration when we feared it wouldn't.

In the album is also a picture of the day he became a keeper. We were college graduates now, and he was in graduate school. I was working, but had a long commute, an old car that was giving me trouble, and a ramen-for-dinner budget. My birthday came and my man handed me a crumpled and dirty paper bag as his gift to me. Inside: dirty and greasy . . . what? The engine parts he'd replaced. Come to find out he'd given me what I needed most: dependability. He'd personally tuned up my car so that I would have a reliable ride. So that every day I could come safely home to the man I loved.

And that I still love, lo these years and sons and many other photographs later.

Christie Ridgway is the author of more than thirty contemporary romances for Avon, Harlequin, Silhouette, and Berkley Books. A California native, she imbues her stories with the flavor of her state. Her current trilogy is set at a Napa Valley winery. Visit www.christieridgway.com to find more about her and her books.

Laura Lee Guhrke

In Praise of Younger Men

I was forty-five years old when I met the love of my life. By then, I'd had plenty of bad dates and my share of heartbreak, and I'd resigned myself to just writing romance, not living it. My friends were used to marking my name down for parties as a solo, and Valentine's Day was just another date on the calendar to me. And when a man sixteen years my junior walked into my life, I just couldn't take him seriously. At first.

We met through friends at a hockey game, and when he invited me to dinner, I was amazed. Why on earth would a man who wasn't even born yet when I started high school want to go out with me? What did we have in common? What could we talk about? I intended to refuse, but my friends accused me of being too narrow-minded, so to prove them wrong, I went out with the guy, and my whole life changed.

When you write romance, you have to put in the grand, sweeping gestures and the passionate declarations, but in real life, true love sneaks up on you, catches you when you're not looking, and teaches you things you didn't even know you needed to learn. Love, Aaron taught me, isn't grand gestures or passionate declarations. It's the little things. It's the insulated coffee cup he gave me because when I'd work long hours at my desk, my coffee would always get cold. It's in the soup he made when I was sick and the flash drive he got to hold all my books. It's how he takes my car in for alignment and he checks the bindings on my skis and he makes sure I eat dinner when I'm in my manic writing phases. And it's in the fact that when the chips were really down, he was my staunchest friend and closest ally, and I know he always will be. I still don't understand quite why he fell in love with me, but I fell in love with him because he taught me what love really is. True love is daily. That's why it's timeless. And that's why it's ageless.

New York Times bestselling author **Laura Lee Guhrke** spent seven years in advertising, had a successful catering business, and managed a construction company before she decided writing novels was more fun. The author of seventeen historical romances, Laura has received many literary awards, including the RITA Award. When she's not writing, Laura spends her time skiing and wakeboarding. She loves hearing from readers, and you may write to her by visiting her website at www.lauralceguhrke.com.

Afterword

Faith, Hope, and Love

Now seems a good time to continue the story about that good-looking bad boy from across the state line that I told you about in my introduction to this book. We dated our senior year in high school and the summer after we graduated. By the time the leaves were turning golden, we knew we had found our soul mates and planned a January wedding. We were blissfully happy as man and wife in our little corner of the world, but it didn't last long.

There was a big, sad war going on in Vietnam, and two months after we were married, my brand-new husband was drafted into the Army. Floyd didn't mind serving his country and in a way was eager to go. Watching him leave that cold, bleak morning was one of the hardest things I've ever had to do. It was difficut for his parents, too, because Floyd had lost a brother in Vietnam just three years before and there was great fear we'd lose him as well.

I'm sure it was due to the prayers offered up by many that Floyd never made it to Vietnam when he was a soldier. The Department of the Army decided they needed him to stay in Ft.

Benning, Georgia, for his two-year stint. Our beautiful daughter was born while we were there, followed by the birth of our son after Floyd was discharged, and we moved back to Alabama. We didn't have much money but we were still crazily in love. I took care of the children and Floyd worked and continued his education. However, my happy life came to a roaring halt when the man I loved with all my heart told me he wanted to leave his safe, comfortable job with Alabama's State Department of Revenue and move to Connecticut. I'm a dyed in the wool Southerner, dropping my consonants when I talk, and saying "Bless your heart" to strangers. How could the love of my life want to move me fifteen hundred miles away from my nearest friend or relative to live in what I considered the highfalutin world of New England?

But the move to what I considered, at the time, the outer banks of the planet, was a blessing in disguise. My husband flourished in his job and the children thrived. I found that being so far away from friends and family gave me freedom to try the wings I'd always had but had never tried to use. For once in my married life, I had time on my hands to do whatever I wanted: get a job, get a college degree, get busy with volunteer work, or write a book.

Write a book?

Yes, I wrote my first book, a romance, in secret while Floyd was at work and the children at school. When it was finished I had to do something with the four-hundred pages; I had to try to sell the book, but first I had to tell my husband I'd written it. It seems odd to me now that I was reluctant to confide in him because our relationship was so close. But with many years to think about that time, I now know the root reason for my concealment was because I feared I wasn't good enough to get published, and if I told him about the book, that meant I'd have to try to sell it. Floyd's love and encouragement enabled me to overcome my hesitancy and I finally told him what I had done. True to his nature, he was thrilled for me and from that very evening when I trusted him with my secret, he has always been my biggest fan, and he has always been the hero in all my books.

It wasn't always smooth sailing for us. We've certainly had our share of ups and downs. But we never allowed anger, complacency, or differences of opinions to weigh us down or tear us apart. We always found a way through faith, hope, and love to reconcile whatever came up and move on.

Acknowledgments

It is with grateful appreciation that I sing the praises of two assistants, Rebecca David and Beth Rains, who helped me keep all sixty-seven authors' stories, bios, and photographs in manageable order. These lovely ladies actually work for my husband, but true hero that he is, he allowed them to devote some of their time to helping me. I also want to give a loud round of applause to the original seventeen authors who wrote their stories for me long before we knew there would be a published book. Joan Johnston, Mary Jo Putney, Stef Ann Holm, Jill Marie Landis, Heather Graham, Kat Martin, Pat Potter, Karen Robards, Linda Lael Miller, Meryl Sawyer, Stella Cameron, Stephanie Bond, Ciji Ware, Nicole Byrd, Rachel Gibson, Jasmine Creswell, Geri Buckley Borcz: stand up and take a bow!

I must also give special thanks to my agent, Celeste Fine, for her interest and belief in this book from the moment I told her about it. And it is with deep gratitude that I say a heartfelt thank you to my editor, Michele Matrisciani, for her expert advice and guidance in making this book come together beautifully. For their help, encouragement, and never failing interest through the years, I salute my local writers' group: Laura Morrigan, Frances Grow, Geri Buckley Borcz, Sandra Shanklin, Hortense Thurman, Liz Graham, Marti Jones, and Dolores Monaco.

Lastly, with loving appreciation I say thank you to my daughter, Charla, who gave me just the pep talk I needed when I thought of giving up on this idea. And it is with endearing thanks to my husband, Floyd, my hero because he has given me my very own happily-ever-after.